Elva Irene McMillan

Lyrics of the West

Elva Irene McMillan

Lyrics of the West

ISBN/EAN: 9783744786676

Printed in Europe, USA, Canada, Australia, Japan

Cover: Foto ©Andreas Hilbeck / pixelio.de

More available books at **www.hansebooks.com**

LYRICS OF THE WEST

BY

ELVA IRENE McMILLAN

G. P. PUTNAM'S SONS

NEW YORK   LONDON

27 WEST TWENTY-THIRD ST.   24 BEDFORD ST., STRAND

The Knickerbocker Press

1899

The Knickerbocker Press, New York

CONTENTS

CONTENTS.

LYRICS OF THE WEST.

THE LAND WHERE DREAMS COME TRUE.

THERE 's a land where deathless flowers
  Breathe their fragrance on the air,
And the little wounded song-bird
  Lives again more glad and fair.
There the stormclouds do not lower,
  For the sky is ever blue,
'T is the place where lovers linger,
  And the land where dreams come true.

There the minstrels songs are singing
  That were left to us unsung,
And the marriage bells are ringing
  That on earth were never rung.
There the jewels flash and sparkle
  For the many, not the few,
And there 's ne'er a wind a-sighing
  In the land where dreams come true.

1

I have seen a little maiden
  Fix her gaze upon the stars,
Then I 've seen her, unsuspecting,
  Turn and grasp the sin that mars.
And the years roll on in sadness,
  And the sky has lost its blue—
Little maiden, stars are shining
  In the land where dreams come true.

Thus we all have seen the shadow,
  And we long for light of day,
Oh, the flowers quickly wither
  That are blooming by the way.
There are voices gently calling,
  Where the music 's ever new,
And there 's ne'er a note of sadness
  In the land where dreams come true.

We are waiting—worn and weary,
  By the river deep and wide,
For the coming of the boatman
  Who shall take us all a ride.
Ah, we 'll sing as we go sailing
  O'er the laughing waters blue,
To the land of blooming flowers,
  And the land where dreams come true.

FROM OUT THE SWEETNESS OF THE PAST.

From out the sweetness of the past,
Those dreams of joy that could not last,
I 've felt a touch that seemed to thrill
Like love's first kiss—Ah, e'en until
From rosy-tinted clouds I dreamed
That cooling waters fell.   It seemed
The zephyrs on the wing were borne
To rend the veil 'twixt night and morn.

Naught but a pile of ashes heaped
On altar where the flame once leaped,
A voice whose tones are oft suppressed,
To still the pain within my breast,
And yet I cling to thee—Oh, stay,
Ye memories, and give, I pray,
Thy touch, nor leave me at the last,
As did the sweetness of the past.

Perchance in fairer worlds than this,
No hand may dash the cup of bliss

From thirsty lips away.   Yet give,
O power divine, all joy—to live
For ages—this to them who sing
As passionless as bird of wing,
But this to me—one hour at last,
From out the sweetness of the past.

LOVE'S YEARNING.

IF it were mine to gather in my hands unfading
flowers;
If it were mine to sing in sweeter tones than mortals sing;
If I could drink of every joy, and stay the fleeting
hours;
If I could change to fairy forms the winds upon
the wing;
Oh, could I all of this and more—all else to me
were given;
If I, whene'er I slept, within an angel's arms
could rest,
I 'd give all these, and then me thinks I 'd know
the bliss of heaven
If I could only lay my head one moment on thy
breast.

Then like the song that sweetly thrilled, then died
while joy imparting,
Yea, like the rose that bloomed to die beneath a
sky most fair,

This moment be as fleeting, yet, within that brief
  space hiding,
  Were more of rapture, more of joy, than love,
    sweet love, can bear.
E'en were I queen of heaven's hosts, of all fair
  beings fairest,
  I yet had not known happiness—I 'd come to
    earth in quest
Of this, my love, and, oh, 't would be the moment
  dearest, rarest,
  If it were mine to lay my head one moment on
    thy breast.

I WILL BE TRUE.

I WILL be true; we 've said good-bye,
We 'll meet no more, love, you and I,
   Let silence keep her royal throne,
   The future shall the past atone,
The coming years may drag or fly,

Like clouds in yonder dismal sky,
Earth's blossoms droop, and fade and die,
   So doth each joy, yet I depone,
      I will be true.

Fond memories of the past draw nigh,
When wrapped in slumber I shall lie;
   Bring back the one I love, alone,
   Whom death nor demons shall dethrone
From my true heart—we 've said good-bye,
      I will be true.

A FADED ROSE.

A FADED rose, 't is all thou art,
And yet thou speakest to my heart,
   And what thou sayest none may hear
   Save me alone, and oft a tear
Is in mine eye—we could but part.

Thou gavest me this rose, sweetheart;
I wore it on my breast. Impart
   Sweetness and grace, thou treasure dear,
      A faded rose.

Yes, faded, crumpled rose, ye start
Infinite longings, and the smart
   Of pain ye give, but pain were cheer,
   For love is true, though far or near;
And so I bless, I prize, sweetheart,
      A faded rose.

I LOVE YOU.

I LOVE you, dear one, tell me how
Or why you dare not thus avow
   Your heart to me; you call me fair,
   And gentle words you do not spare,
Before me like a king you bow;

You kiss my lips, my cheeks, my brow,
You press me to your heart, and now
   I listen for these words so dear:
      I love you.

Laud not my beauty—more, allow
My heart to rest, or else endow
   With these three words I long to wear,
   Like jewels on my soul; forbear
All things to say, or whisper now:
      I love you.

TO LIVE.

"IT is not all of life to live,"
    A precious gem of poet's thought,
The numbered years we sadly give,
    And learn to live.

I have not lived in vain if I
    Have offered but one kindly word,
Have kissed away while moments fly
    One weary sigh.

Or if, perchance, for one in need
    Of mercy and a helping hand,
I lend my own—no censure heed,
    But sow good seed.

It may be when the day is drear,
    I pluck a rose of brightest hue,
And let it bear a ray of cheer
    To one most dear.

To pray for some poor heart, forgive,
    If one have wronged thee, aye, to sing
Tho' tears are in thine eyes, believe
    'T is this to live.

SWEETEST WORDS.

THE sweetest words of mother, friend, or brother,
  The dearest words of lover fond and true,
The words that speak the heart, imparting gladness,
  Rich jewels like the stars in heaven's blue;
That fall upon the ear like psalms at twilight,
  And calm the soul like carol of the birds,
The sweetest words may not be these, " I love
    you,"
  " God bless you," softly spoken—sweetest words.

WHAT ARE THE WILD WAVES SAYING?

WHAT are the wild waves saying?
  List to the song at sea,
Perchance a golden message
  Lies in the sea for thee.
Hark! 't is a gentle murmur,
  Breathed as a breath divine,
Over the waves of ocean,
  Into this heart of mine.

What are the wild waves saying?
  When o'er their foaming crest,
Gaily the proud ships sailing,
  Glide like a thing at rest.
Waken! the wild waves whisper,
  Waken! ye souls who sleep,
Sing while the days are fleeting,
  Love is an ocean deep.

This, too, the waves are telling,
  " Ships that pass in the night

Greet one another passing,''
　List to the waves to-night.
Only a kind word spoken,
　Out on the sea of life,
Lifted a fallen brother,
　Led him from sin and strife.

What are the wild waves saying ?
　Look unto God and live!
Follow the paths of virtue,
　If thou art wronged, forgive.
Breathe not the breath of slander,
　Dare to do right alway,
Ever the wild waves whisper—
　Live but to love and pray.

WHEN LOVE SHALL COME.

SOME day shall love at my chamber knock,
And I shall at once unbolt the door,
And bid him enter and find sweet rest,
And pillow his head on my snowy breast.
O God, I have kept my heart from sin,
'That a pure, true love it were mine to give,
I have bathed my soul in the light of heaven,
That love might be held in constancy.
And my heart like a lyre whose strings unswept
Sing out 'neath the snow-white fingers—waits
For the touch of flame—oh, infinite bliss,
In dreams I have thrilled 'neath the lover's kiss.
Come, love, to me in the soft twilight,
I yearn for the sound of thy light footfall.
Would'st thou wake my soul with a pure desire ?
Would'st thou drink to the full the sweets of love ?
'Then be thou as pure, as worthy be
As e'er in my waiting dream thou art;
For love to be constant must be pure,
And love is immortal only so.
Ah, who can a great soul-passion feel ?

Not she who hath drunk from many a cup,
Whose soul is dead to a noble trust,
But she whose thought at the midnight hour
Is purified in the light of prayer.
When my king shall come I have been true,
And I have no fear when his lips touch mine;
Let me drink from his lips the nectar sweet,
And lie on his breast in pure delight,
Yea, know that I 've hidden within my heart
Joys that are sweetest for him alone.
Love is devotion, it hath been said,
Another hath named it sympathy,
Methinks 't is a dream of bliss, a joy
By mortal man never yet defined.
But this I know, that with outstretched arms
I wait to receive this king of bliss,
My heart all tuned to his lightest touch,
My soul swept clear of all baser thought;
And ever he comes, I live to say,
I 've waited thy coming and been true.

THE CHILDREN'S HOUR.

NIGHT is falling round the cottage,
   It is now the children's hour;
Tiny voices laugh and prattle,
   While the mother's kisses shower
Over each fair brow their blessings,
   Mother's kisses—what delight!
Who like she can sing so sweetly,
   Who so brightly smile to-night?

Seated in the dim old parlor,
   At the organ, list, she sings,
And the little ones around her,
   Seem to hear the fairy wings.
While the voice so sweet and gentle
   Breathes its beauty on the air,
'T is a picture for an artist,
   For an artist's theme most fair.

Song is ended, lamps are lighted,
   And the curtains have been drawn,
There 's no sound of baby laughter
   Now upon the grassy lawn.

Little ones are, oh, so quiet,
 List'ning to the precious Word,
Ere the good-nights have been spoken,
 And they kneel before the Lord.

I 'm a friend in this glad circle,
 Oft I join in prayer and song,
Sometimes tell a gladsome tale, and
 Thus the children's hour prolong.
But more often am I dreaming
 I 'm a painter, bless'd alway,
Just to paint this wife and babies,
 In these scenes at close of day.

When each little prayer is finished
 Comes a scene more bless'd to me
Than to roam in fields Elysian,
 Sipping sweets from every tree.
Then the mother brings her baby
 For the father's kiss.   Oh, there
Is a picture for a painter,
 With a theme of all most fair.

Little ones are tucked so neatly
 In a dainty, snowy bed,

And again each parent kisses
   Little Rosa, Will, and Ned.
Then I 've watched the tear-drops falling,
   While the lips have framed a smile,
As the mother bent above them,
   Dreaming of the after while.

I have brought each scene before you
   That I see at close of day,
In this home where love is shining
   Brighter than the sun's own ray.
But of all the treasured pictures
   While the mother kneels in prayer,
Babe in arms, beside its cradle,
   This must be of all most fair.

SAILING.

Life is a great, great ocean, dear,
  Over her bosom glides
Beautiful forms that as swiftly go
  As the king of the night wind rides.
And the skies are fair and the songs are rare,
  And we sip from the fount of pleasure,
While over the sea of life we sail,
  And hide in the heart love's treasure.

Out on the great, wide ocean, dear,
  Two little boats are sailing,
Fate, who is king of the land and sea,
  Shall guide to the port unfailing.
And it may be, dear,—in the thought there 's
      cheer,—
  They shall glide alongside each other,
Oh, it may be, dear, in a golden hour,
  They shall meet, though they part forever.

MY TREASURE IS WITH GOD.

THE snow lies deep on yonder little mound,
    I do not weep;
Death hath not robbed me, I have found
    The way to God since baby came
    And taught me how to breathe His name,
    Then fell asleep.

MY GIFTS.

I SEEK not jewels rare nor perfumes sweet
    This Christmas day,
But, Father, kneeling at Thy feet,
  A firmer trust is all my need,
  A purer heart, for this I plead;
    These give, I pray.

FORGIVENESS.

You go your way, dear one, and I,
 Altho' you made my heart to bleed,
Am praying you 'll return; maybe,
 Your soul not yet has felt the need
Of pardon and of peace, and yet
 I long to fold you to my breast,
And kiss your eyes, your lips, and bid
 Your wand'ring spirit find sweet rest.

You do not like to say, " forgive,"
 You fear to come lest I 'll reprove;
The years go by, and you forget
 I gave to you my soul's best love.
And think you I 'd be stern and cold ?
 Ah, little do you know my heart,
I 've all forgotten now, dear one,
 But that as friends we did not part.

If I were you, and mine the wrong,
 Before to-morrow's setting sun,

I 'd kneel before you, dear, and plead
　　Your pardon for the evil done.
And yet I would not have you ask—
　　What! need you ask ? does love still live ?
Dear heart, I love you—all forget,
　　And sweet it is just to forgive.

TO LOVE.

IF I were dead, thy kiss alone
  Would call me back to life,
And if I slept where demons moan,
  Where all the air with sin is rife,
    And thou wert passing by,
To see thy face would all atone,
    My soul would reach the sky.

For, says the Good Book, " God is love,"
  Ah, then, 't is plain to see
Where love may be—but need I prove
  'T is heaven at once where love may be ?
    Oh, sweet, sweet love, abide
With me, and to the courts above
    I shall not be denied.

SWEET ROSES.

MELT upon my lips, O thou
   Queen of all fair flowers,
Leave thy perfume on my breath
   Through life's golden hours.
Whisper to my soul—thou art
   Mercy's kisses given
By the dear, kind hand of God,
   From the sweets of heaven.

Ah, methinks when first the earth,
   Clothed in bloom and beauty,
Threw her kisses to the sun,
   Knew that joy was duty.
Then an angel dropped a smile
   To the earth—it melted,
Budded, bloomed a pure white rose,
   And, ere it had wilted,

Love was pledged to all mankind
   By its pure white petals,

By its perfume, wondrous rare,
   Dripped from heaven's portals.
Then the red rose bloomed—passion's
   Ruddy face in nature—
Kissing us with her dear lips,
   Thrilling life with pleasure.

Pink roses came—enchanting, fair,
   Then man tuned his lyre,
Dreamed his dream and gave the world
   Strains from heaven's choir.
Then the little sweet wild rose,
   Blooming on the plain,
Grew for beauty's sake unseen,
   Lived, but not in vain.

Roses sweet, oh, joy ye give!
   Teach me thine adorning;
Ah, 't is but the breath of God,
   Breathed when first the morning
Waves her banners to the sun!
   Life that nothing loses
By its swift decay—loved, pure,
   Joy of all—sweet roses.

MARY MAGDALENE.

[Charles F. Deems, in his *Light of the Nations*, speaking
of Mary Magdalene, says: " Here is one of those unhappy
cases in history in which some misapprehension has occurred
which has succeeded in branding a name with an undeserved
infamy and perpetuating it through generations. In her real
life she was lifted to a heaven of love ; in history, she has
been cast down to a hell of infamy. Let her be restored.
The truth does restore her. The friend of Jesus was a
blessed saint."]

STRIKE the harp with gentle fingers,
　　Softly touch the strings to-night;
Let me sing, and if there lingers
　　Sadness in the strain so bright,
Drop a tear; I sing to tell thee
　　Story sweet as ever told,
Of the wondrous love of Mary,
　　Mary Magdalene of old.

Friend of Jesus, saintly Mary,
　　See her kneeling at the cross,
While her heart in silent passion
　　Burns with torture in her loss.

And He died—she saw Him buried,
  Knew not He would rise again,
Fondest hope of Him had perished
  In His grave—such was her pain.

To the sepulchre she hastened,
  When the Sabbath day was done,
And her tears like rain were falling,
  She was counting one by one
Dying words that He had uttered,
  Seemed His every groan she heard,
For she loved the sad, sweet music
  Of each well-remembered word.

But the sepulchre was empty,
  Angel forms were standing there,
Whom she heeded not, but yielded
  Once again to dark despair.
Jesus came, He gently murmured,
  In the tones she knew so well,
One word—" Mary,"—but it thrilled her
  Back to consciousness—she fell

At His feet, she dared not touch Him,
  Yet her gentle heart did yearn

Just to clasp His feet, to touch them
 With her lips—her heart did burn.
And methinks when He had left her,
 Oft she kissed the hallowed spot
Where He stood, while there recalling
 Saintly words—these: " Touch me not."

Oh, how well she loved her Healer !
 'T was a love more sweet, more true
Than the dews that fall at twilight,
 Than the light in heaven's blue.
And He loved her as no other—
 Sweetest story ever told—
Of the Saviour's love to Mary,
 Mary Magdalene of old.

FIRELIGHT REVERIES.

When the night has drawn her curtains,
　　And the candles have been lit;
When you sit you down in silence,
　　And you dream, and nod, and knit;
Know ye not your home so happy,
　　Free from every troubled air,
Shall one day be dark and gloomy,
　　When Death's angel enters there ?

And my sister, sweet and gentle,
　　Loved and cherished far and near,
Have you not a friend in sorrow,
　　Who would prize a word of cheer ?
One whose lonely heart would cherish
　　Little whisperings of love ?
White-winged messengers—oh, send them;
　　Gladly flies the carrier dove.

Drop your knitting, then, 't is better,
　　With your pen and paper write,

You have labored through the morning,
   It will give sweet rest to-night
Just to pen some words of kindness,
   That may lift a load of care;
If your heart o'erflows with gladness,
   Give to one less glad a share.

Have a smile for those who love thee,
   Have a tear for those who hate;
When a wayworn traveller cometh,
   Open wide the vineyard gate.
And when darkness spreads her banner
   'Neath the twinkling stars above,
Write those messages of comfort,
   Seal them with the kiss of love.

MY KANSAS HOME.

THE dear old farm I yearn to see,
  Whose fields my bare feet loved to roam,
The place my chidhood loved the best,
  My Kansas home.

When but a tiny, wayward thing,
  I loved to sail the prairie sea,
And sing the grand old granger songs,
  So dear to me.

The curling buff'lo grass was fair
  To me as fields of clover bloom,
It carpeted my play-house floor
  In every room.

And what cared I if 'long the trail
  The Indians were wont to stray,
They harmed me not—oh, happy time,
  My youth's bright day.

You tell me that the sunbeams burned
  The very seed in prairie sea;

3

Ah, well, if that be false or true,
    'T is naught to me.

And oft I hear you, laughing, say,
    That long ago the winds were wild,
Perhaps that may be true, but then
    I was a child.

To-day the dear old home is changed,
    Perhaps I would not know the place,
Could I go back, old paths I think
    I could not trace.

And yet how sweet to dream of thee,
    Beneath the blue of heaven's dome!
Thy memory is a joy to me,
    My Kansas home.

WHEN YOU VISIT ME IN DREAMS.

SOMETIMES in the hour before the dawn,
  From a golden cup my spirit sips,
For 't is then you come at the break of day,
  And I wake with your kiss upon my lips.
And I know not whether I 'm blest or no,
  For your lips on mine bring back my pain,
And yet I 'm glad when the day is done,
  I may hold you close in my dreams again.

O God ! that you 'd clasp me to your breast,
  And breathe in my face your sweet, warm breath,
And speak my name in the tones I love,
  Then float with me thro' the gates of death.
For I would not wake from my dreams, dear heart,
  For after the sweet dream joys are o'er,
My heart so yearns, like a fretting child,
  To creep back into your arms once more.

THE LITTLE ONES.

" OH, your mamma is so nice! "
  'T was a baby voice I heard,
Speaking to my youngest darling,
  And I treasured each fond word.
'T was a day when things unkind,
  Said of me I 'd chanced to hear,
When the venom of a falsehood
  Pierced me with its poisoned spear.

Then I kissed the precious child,
He looked up in my face and smiled,
" Always I think you 're so good,"
Said the little one.   Ah, would
Envy's verdict nearer be
Fair and just and right ?   I see
He who with joy life's journey runs,
Doth heed love's voice—the little ones.

TO THE VIOLINIST.

SOFTLY, sweetly, grand, majestic,
   Float the tones upon the air,
Unto one of love they whisper,
   To another breathe a prayer.
What the tale, O strange musician,
   Thou art seeking to declare ?
Dost thou tell of joy or sadness ?
   Are thy visions marred or fair ?

Who can tell, who can interpret
   What thou sayest ?   Enter in
To thy secret, hidden meaning,
   Dreamer with the violin ?
For thy tones are sweet, yea, sweeter
   Than in dreams the lover's kiss,
And anon they trill and tremble,
   Like the song of birds we miss.

Then the tones die out in sadness,
   Naught save longing and regret

Speak the heart, for at thy bidding
  Memory awakes—and yet
Would I hide within the casket
  Of my life of yesterday
Dreams that vanished with the waking ?
  Still forget to love and pray ?

Ah, I caught the white-winged message,
  Like the poet's jewelled lance,
Higher rose the strains majestic,
  Then in one swift, burning glance
Spoke he all his soul ; and never
  In a world of strife and sin,
Shall I meet again the dreamer
  With the dear, loved violin.

WHEN SCHOOL BEGINS.

THE names must all be written
　　In school-books neat and new,
And covers made to keep them,
　　And pencils sharpened, too;
For little sons and daughters
　　We love these things to do.

There 's Tom's name to be written
　　In all his books—that 's eight,
And Lizzie's six, then Freddie's,
　　I 'll print it on his slate.

How short a time it seemeth
　　Since I, too, was a child,
And father brought my school-books,
　　With joy my heart was wild;
To study was my pleasure,
　　And hope my hours beguiled.

They all come back so plainly,
　　Those days so far away,

When mother wrote my name in
  My school-books; and to-day

Another memory waketh,
  There 's one less name to write
Than when last year they brought me
  Their books; sad thoughts bedight
The teardrops, how I 'll miss him!
  One less to kiss good-bye,
When off to school the children
  At morn and noon shall hie.

And lonely here I 'm watching,
  Lest little feet should roam,
And 'mid the tears I 'm praying
  Beneath God's fair blue dome,
That when life's school is ended,
  We all shall meet at home.

MY OFFERING.

I ONCE thought life all beauty,
    Her paths the ways of peace,
The winds so sweetly, softly sighed,
    In all their glad release.

And then I brought my offering
    Unto our God; my prayers
And lovely thoughts I gave Him,
    And my heart knew naught of cares.

Life's morn I brought to Him
    A heart that loved to sing;
Life's beauties all I sought, then gave
    To God my offering.

I lived, and then came duty
    A-wooing at my feet,
Although his pleadings men despise,
    To me his voice was sweet.

Perchance he 'd be unkind if one
    Should loiter by the way,

And yet since I have loved him,
  I 've learned aright to pray.

And now I shall present
  The gifts I have to bring—
Life's duties.   Thus I yield to God
  My heart's best offering.

THOU HAST A HOPE.

THOU hast a hope within thy breast,
  A cherished, sweet desire;
Nay, more it is, though well concealed,
  A deathless flame of fire.

The gods have kissed thy ruby lips,
  Their gift has left a madness
To tear the veil from poet's heart,
  And sing the world thy gladness.

Thy song is sung and dies unheard,
  The world is full of beauty;
But sing again, be not cast down,
  Sing on and do thy duty.

Have faith in God, have faith in man,
  Have faith in efforts given,
Keep smiling on, the darkest clouds
  Shall flee, by sunshine driven.

43

The soul that 's brave, that dares to try,
 For him the stars are shining;
Then sing, I pray, the poet's lay,
 And cease thy heart's repining.

OH, THAT WITH THE GENTLE POETS.

Oh, that with the gentle poets
   I could claim the humblest place,
For I 'd sing not of the angels,
   But of Nature and her grace.
I would tell you what the flowers
   In their simple language say,
When they bloom in perfect beauty,
   Bloom, then fade, and pass away.

I would listen to the birdlings,
   And interpret their sweet song,
For I know they sing of mercy
   And of love the summer long.
And in every gentle breeze I
   Think I 'd hear an angel's song,
I 'd commune with Nature's God, and
   Paint not lust and earthly wrong.

I 'd not picture ugly storm-clouds,
   I 'd not put in rhyme things vile,
But I 'd seek to draw a picture
   Of an infant child's first smile.

I would teach that to be happy,
　　Man should live to love and pray,
He should live to bless another,
　　Singing duty's song each day.

Look! the lovely, leafy woodland
　　Opens wide her arms of cheer,
If you yield to her embraces,
　　You will find that God is near.
If you listen He will whisper,
　　That in Nature He has given
Singing birds and blooming flowers,
　　As a tiny glimpse of heaven.

Yes, if with the gentle poets
　　I could claim the humblest place,
I would paint for you fair Nature,
　　In her true and perfect grace.
And in my verse you then should hear
　　Little children laugh and sing,
Ah, I 'd lead the world to worship
　　At the feet of Christ, my King.

"HE DON'T KNOW ME."

[The following verses were suggested by a visit of mercy paid by the writer to a poor abandoned woman in her prison cell.]

DARK is the dungeon where she hides,
    Crushed by her sin and shame,
Fair is her face and young is she,
    Lost, but for her Christ came.
One who has felt the touch of God,
    Tells of His love so free,
Whispers of pardon, but said she:
    "Woman, He don't know me."

Once in the years not long gone by,
    One little babe just born,
Nestled close to its mother's heart,
    Glad was its young life's morn.
Ah, seems to me I hear them yet,
    Prayers by that mother given,
"Father, oh lead my baby's feet
    Straight to the gates of heaven."

Years roll away, that mother died;
    Sin claimed that life so fair,
Now she is sinking 'neath her shame,
    Filled with a dark despair.
Thus when these words were said to her,
    " Jesus is seeking thee,"
Melted to tears she sadly said,
    " Woman, He don't know me."

Ye who are mothers, do ye hear
    This poor girl's sad refrain ?
Press to your heart your daughters fair,
    Shield them from sin and pain.
Yet as ye would they were done by,
    So unto others be,
Who in their shame hide from their God,
    Saying, " He don't know me."

Ye who are 'neath the blood of Christ,
    Blow ye your trumpets, blow!
Bring the poor lost ones home to God,
    Go to the desert, go!
Can ye who feel the love of **God**
    Setting your spirits free,
Go on rejoicing while lost souls
    Cry out, " He don't know me " ?

Oh, for the hearts that feel the cost
   Christ for the lost ones gave,
The hearts that care not where they go,
   God's erring ones to save.
Washed in the blood of Christ from sin
   And shame, they shall be free,
Our Saviour came to save the lost
   Who say, " He don't know me."

4

"GIVE ME THINE HEART."

" Give me thine heart," the dear Redeemer said
All day the words rang thro' my aching head,
   At night in dreams the pleading voice I heard,
   And sought to still it, for each tender word
Was torture to my soul. At last I said,

I will be thankful for my daily bread,
I 'll help the needy, kneel down by my bed,
Repeat my prayers—no longer say, dear Lord,
   " Give me thine heart."

One day I wept beside my precious dead,
All hope, it seemed, from out my life had fled,
   I knelt to pray, but like a wounded bird,
   I think the Father reckoned me—I heard,
And all my being thrilled when now He said,
   " Give me thine heart."

MY YOUTH.

If I had beauty, love, and health,
And fame, and every joy, forsooth,
I 'd give them all and count it wealth,
If only I might keep my youth.

MEDITATION.

OH, would that spring
   Were here with birds and flowers,
Green grass and leafy trees,
   And sunlit show'rs.

'T is then I long
   To leave the town, and flee
To Nature's fond embrace,
   In shady lea.

And there unsought,
   My hiding-place unknown,
I would commune with God,
   Sweetly alone.

My soul finds peace,
   By Nature's moods caressed,
On her God's finger writes
   Eternal rest.

MY ANSWER.

You ask me why I love the Spring so well,
  That maid whose mood brings forth or wind or
      rain;
  You love Queen Summer best—her golden grain,
Her smiling skies have cast you 'neath a spell.
But I love best the first sweet notes that tell
  That Winter 's fled. Ere flowers graced the plain
  I knew you first, and, dear, those days remain
Of all my life the best—then silence fell
Between us when the Autumn days drew near.
  It needs no word to prove your heart is true,
And yet your silence stole the Winter's cheer,
  My heart rejoiced at bidding him adieu
To welcome back the Spring-time, ah, and then,
When Summer roses bloom we 'll meet again.

WHO SAILS WITH ME?

Who sails with me ?—my ship hath charms,
And sails a sea that nothing harms;
   The ships that rest upon her breast,
   By winds and waves at once caressed.
The storm may sweep the sea, alarms
Be given—fear thou not—my arms
Are strong to guide to port.   Ye storms,
   Ride on ! my ship is safest, best—
      Who sails with me ?

On board my vessel, who conforms
To all the Captain's rules disarms
   The very prince of darkness.   Guessed
   Beneath whose flag we sail ?—then rest—
King Love our pilot is—naught harms
      Who sails with me.

I WILL LISTEN.

I WILL listen in the morning
  For Thy dear and tender voice,
And I 'll follow where Thou leadest,
  For I 've made Thy paths my choice.
I will listen; Thou wilt call me
  When the way is dark and drear,
And I need so much to listen
  Lest Thy voice I may not hear.

I will listen in the tempest,
  And I 'll hear thy " Peace, be still,"
If my cross seem hard to carry,
  I will hear, " Not as I will."
When Thy cross was, oh, so heavy,
  Thou didst humbly, sweetly say,
" Not as I will, but as Thou wilt,"
  Help me thus, my Lord, to pray.

THE LOVE OF GOD.

You have seen the clouds when they drift apart,
  Let the lovely sunshine through;
Thro' the clouds of life I have seen God's love
  Like the sunlight warm and true.

WHEN I MEET THEE.

When I meet thee,
Shall I greet thee
    With a sigh ?
Shall I turn away my face
That the blushes sure will grace,
So that love you cannot trace
    In my eye ?

Ah, I 'll greet thee
When I meet thee
    By and by,
With a glance that speaks the love
Angels whisper from above,
Love is ever true to love—
    Crowned am I.

WHILE THE BABY SLEEPS.

On a downy bed of snow
   Little baby lies;
How I 'd love to kiss him! but
   If I do he cries.
So I turn to leave him there,
But I kneel and breathe a prayer
That the angels hover near
   Where my baby lies.

IT IS SWEET TO LOVE.

It is sweet to love when the summer day
Bids the earth be glad and the heart be gay;
When the darkness sheds not a single ray,
   Oh, then it is sweet to love.

But the summer day cometh not to stay,
And its sunshine yields to the winter gray;
In the night of life shall the heart be gay ?
   Ah, yes, it is sweet to love.

THE FUTURE.

THE beautiful future,
  She beckons to me;
She bids me press onward
  Her glory to see.
I 'll rest me for aye on her bosom of love,
I 'll gaze on her beauty, with her I will rove;
I 'll sing to the future a song of true love,
For, ah, she is singing to me.

LITTLE GRACE.

I THINK of her with dancing curls,
　　The light of childhood in her face,
The loved of all, both boys and girls,
　　My little school-mate—Grace.

The brightest scholar in our set,
　　Ah me, she gave us all a race
To keep with her—who could forget
　　Dear, laughing little Grace ?

And then before we reached our teens,
　　My parents brought me to the West,
And, friends, you all know what it means
　　To leave one dearer than the rest.

Long years rolled by, her face alone
　　Was written on my memory;
It seemed naught could to me atone
　　If I no more her face might see.

So after many years had fled,
　　I went back to the old home place;

When there at once to friends I said,
  " Tell me of little Grace.

" Wait, does she live, and is she here ?
  In all these years I 've had no trace,
What! you must surely know her, dear,
  My little school-mate, Grace.

" My God! What can it be ? Altho'
  You weep and turn from me your face,
I pray you tell if aught you know
  Of her, my playmate, Grace.

" What 's this you say, been dead for years ?
  What! died in shame and in disgrace ?
My God! that can't be true—my ears
  Are hard of hearing, little Grace.

" I 'll not believe this thing you 've guessed,
  This hell-born tale, sir, you shall prove!
The babe sleeps on the mother's breast ?
  It may be true, great God above!

" Well, if you speak the truth, go on,
  And spare me not, though hard the blow,

You tell me that another won
  My Grace's heart ?   My friend, no, no!

" We were but children then, 't is true,
  But she had promised she 'd be mine,
I loved her—God! she loved me, too,
  I saw it in her bright eyes shine.

" Come, take me to her grave—when there
  If this you say, it must be truth.
Oh, lost, lost, lost, my child so fair,
  Lost, lost in all her bloom and youth.

" You say before she died, for peace
  And pardon she was heard to call,
And God in mercy did release
  Her soul, forgave her errors all."

She sleeps now in an unmarked grave,
  Her little one upon her breast,
When dying cried, " He came to save—
  Blest Jesus," then she sank to rest.

And he who wrecked her life still lives,
  And he may face a smiling world,

While all the scorn the cold world gives
　　At little Grace is hurled.

But sleep on in thy narrow bed,
　　With naught to mar thy perfect rest;
I 'll plant sweet flowers at thy head,
　　Sleep on—God knoweth best.

God called thee home, and I shall live—
　　No matter how—a little space;
I love thee, and I all forgive,
　　My own dear little Grace.

WHEN LOVE IS YOUNG AND LIFE IS FAIR.

How sweet the joyous dreams of youth!
    Who would not welcome from the past
Those dreams again—ah, who, in truth,
    Would waken from those dreams at last ?
When happy hearts are blind, indeed,
    To shadows creeping everywhere,
How sweet, I say, love's golden meed,
    When love is young and life is fair.

How laughing girls will gaily sing,
    While tripping o'er the grassy lea,
They vie in song with birds of wing,
    And ring the joy bells on life's sea.
And, oh, the song is sweet if sung
    By lips that oft have breathed a prayer,
For all will sing when love is young,
    And all will laugh when life is fair.

Methinks 'tis best in youth's fair day,
    To sweetly sing and not to sigh,

5

65

And blest to learn to love and pray
  While youth's bright days are going by.
And when I 'm old and bent, and turned
  To silver is my golden hair,
I 'll still sing on, for I have learned
  Love 's ever young, life 's always fair.

MOTHERHOOD.

Of all the good and precious gifts,
  From God, the Father, given,
The blessed gift of motherhood
  Hath drawn us nearest heaven.

The angels ever hover round
  The infant at the breast,
Ah, a mother should be holy,
  Bless'd of God, so truly bless'd.

' T is a mighty trust—O Father,
  May we ever faithful prove,
Guide aright these priceless jewels,
  Walk with Thee in faith and love.

WHOM ANGELS CROWNED.

I was weary with life's trials,
   And I thought 't would give release
To my mind to roam in dreamland,
   Breathe its vesper airs of peace.
But there came not when I sought it,
   Sweet forgetfulness so dear,
And I could not banish sorrow,
   Nor encourage thoughts of cheer.

While I lay and wondered idly,
   If the lost chord should be found,
What would be its note of sweetness,
   Where all notes had dismal sound,
Hark! to me is borne in beauty,
   On the balmy evening air,
Song my little girl is singing,
   Like an angel bright and fair.

While I listened came a vision,
   And I closed my weary eyes,
Thus to gaze upon the beauty
   That the spirit eye espies.

And the voice sang on in sweetness,
  While the heavenly host drew near,
Then grew dimmer, weaker, fainter,
  Till it passed away in cheer.

And I looked, and lo! an angel
  From the great white throne of God,
Wearing crown of wond'rous beauty,
  Having in his hand a rod,
Stood and said in tones of music:
  " We will crown our queen for aye,
Who will be the Queen of Heaven ?
  Let her make her plea to-day."

Then before him came a maiden,
  Who was gentle, sweet, and fair,
And her young life had been given
  To the lost in dark despair;
Came the woman who had beauty,
  Came the one whose plea was fame,
Came the woman in whose life had
  Never burned one thought of shame.

And among them came a woman,
  Not bedecked with jewels rare,

But she bore the name of Mother
    On a crescent in her hair.
And she said, " The King of Heaven
    Granted me the gift divine,
When He deemed me to be worthy
    And a little babe was mine.

" I have heard her sing, and angels
    Hearing, too, drew near to bless;
As I 've tried to lead her footsteps,
    God has given His caress.
I can love as doth no angel
    Never bless'd with mother love."
Then the angels shouted, " Crown her
    Queen of all the hosts above."

And the vision passed—I wakened—
    Hear the sweet voice singing yet,
And the long-lost chord is given
    With no discord of regret.
Can it be that life seemed dreary,
    And this sweet-voiced child is mine ?
Let me sing, rejoice, be holy,
    For the crown of crowns is mine.

I LOVE TO HEAR YOU WHISTLE WHEN
YOU 'RE COMING.

OH, I love to hear you whistle
　　When you 're coming home at night,
Though the way be dark and dismal,
　　Or the stars are shining bright.
Ah, 't is true you did not know it,
　　But it thrills me with delight,
If I hear you gaily whistle
　　When you 're coming home at night.

In this world of sin and sorrow,
　　There are haunts to lure the gay,
And I would not have you venture
　　Where you would not dare to pray.
Then I listen in the silence
　　For your footstep quick and light,
And ere long I hear you whistle,
　　When you 're coming home at night.

If I 'm waiting in the darkness—
　　For a mother waits, you know—

And the dismal wind is sighing,
  And the clock is ticking slow,
All the singing of the angels
  Could not give me such delight
As the music of your whistle,
  When you 're coming home at night.

For I know your mind is merry,
  And I know your heart is gay,
And I 'm sure you 've not been walking
  In the paths that lead astray.
If your heart had lost its music,
  And your soul had lost its sight,
You would never come a-whistling
  When you 're coming home at night.

NEARER MY GOD TO THEE.

" NEARER my God to Thee,
　　Nearer to Thee,"
Oh, I have wandered far,
　　So far from Thee.
Yet how I long to flee,
Flee from my sin to Thee;
Open Thy arms to me,
　　Mercy I cry.

Now let Thy precious love
　　Thrill me again,
Forget that I was weak,
　　Fell into sin.
Jesus, I yearn to be
Drawn close again to Thee,
Clings my poor heart to Thee,
　　Save, or I die.

" Nearer my God to Thee,
　　Nearer to Thee,"
Weeping I seek Thy arms,
　　Open for me.

Now through Thy love to me
My life I yield to Thee,
Oh, I 'll stay close to Thee,
   Love is my tie.

WHY ?

THE kiss the hungry heart so craves
   May be withheld, and other lips
Be pressed to ours.   Life's cup of joy
   Is only filled to him who dips
At troubling of the waters.   Come,
   Ye white-winged fairies, hither fly
And show me since this thing be true,
   The secret of it—tell me why.

Ah, tell me why the cup of joy
   Is empty ere we learn to drink;
Why roses wither in the hand;
   Why life sits on death's river brink;
But most of all, pray tell me why
   The blossoms loved are out of reach,
Like far-off worlds of which we dream,
   Who 'll answer why, who this can teach ?

Why is King Love so blind a king ?
   Why is the Queen of Love so sad ?
One kiss Love pressed upon her lips,
   Enough to make the gods go mad!

75

Is love the fairest thing of earth ?
The purest thing in earth or sky ?
Then give me love, I humbly plead,
It may not be—O God! then why ?

DROP A TEAR FOR ME.

Said a youth who loved a maiden,
  " Fairest one, you bid me go
And forget. Ah, then, farewell, love ";
  Then he said in accents low,
" Give your fairest smiles to others
  Who are happy, and will see;
But for me, my heart is breaking,
  Drop a tear for me.

" When you sing, ah, happy maiden,
  Angels fair bedight your song,
When you smile I think the fairies
  Scatter stars your path along.
I had hoped to tune my lyre
  To your notes so glad and free,
Now I can but ask, in pity,
  Drop a tear for me."

Said a beautiful young daisy,
  As she bloomed amid the grass,
" I will tell a tale of gladness
  To the weary ones who pass."

But a wrong, a wayward footstep,
   Crushed her life so fair to see,
With her tale untold she murmured,
   " Drop a tear for me."

Said a maiden who had wandered
   Far from home and love and right,
And was groping in the darkness,
   Where was not one ray of light,
" If I could forget—oh, pity,
   Cursed with sin and memory,
If I could forget!   O fair one,
   Drop a tear for me."

Said a bent old man who trembled,
   As he stood behind the bars,
Gazing upward to the heavens,
   Counting one by one the stars,
" All my life did sin pursue me,
   From his clutch I ne'er was free,
I have struggled—don't condemn, but
   Drop a tear for me."

We are told to scatter roses,
   Told to laugh and sing, be gay;

Told the world has need of gladness,
   But no need of tears, they say.
Yet there is no heart so joyous,
   Not a life so glad and free,
But some day will sadly murmur,
   " Drop a tear for me."

There 's no wayward one so sinful,
   But that mercy should be given,
Smiles are lost sometimes, but ever
   To the heart our tears are driven.
Let us gather up the tear-drops
   That have fallen by the way,
They as gems shall sparkle ever,
   In the land of perfect day.

GONE BEFORE.

[Lines on the death of Miss Nellie Bixler, who died at Lyons, Kansas, August 5, 1896.]

"For me to live is Christ, and to die is gain."—
Philippians, i., 21.

WE have seen a life of beauty,
　　Fairer than the sweetest flower,
Gently pass beyond our vision,
　　Leaving, like a summer shower,
Brighter sunshine, greater beauty,
　　While we gaze through tears of pain,
On the perfect life now vanished,
　　Yet, ere long we 'll meet again.

Still she points the way to heaven,
　　Gentle maiden, pure and fair,
Queen of all the holy graces,
　　Patient, knowing not despair;
And she passed beyond the shadow,
　　Into pure and perfect day,
And her holy life allures us
　　To her home not far away.

Yes, we weep, but she forbids us;
  Queenly Nell, so young and true,
Stands beside the great white throne, and
  Beckons, friends, to me and you.
And her voice in sweetest music,
  Sings to us from heaven's shore,
" When the trump of God has sounded,
  We shall meet to part no more."
  6

BALLAD OF FAITH AND LOVE.

I DO not know what love may be,
   Could I define the gift so rare,
I think e'en then ye could not see
   Love's beauty all, so I forbear.
I cannot tell how man may dare
   To seek the Father at His throne,
Yet something seems to whisper there,
   The heart of God is love alone.

But this I know, the winds blow free,
   And songs of beauty kiss the air,
And sweet birds sing their songs of glee,
   And flowers bloom, yea, everywhere.
And so, you see, I 've learned to wear
   The wreath of faith; to me is shown
That God is love—this can ye bear ?
   The heart of God is love alone.

Out on life's great blue surging sea
   We gaily sail while skies are fair,

Ah, who shall pilot to the lee
  Our vessel ?—storms rise unaware.
A friend's best love may prove a snare,
  The heart grows faint, and yet unknown,
He leads whose wondrous works declare
  The heart of God is love alone.

ENVOY.

I sing of faith, and love, and prayer,
  O Father, may Thy love be known
To all the world—this be my care—
  The heart of God is love alone.

UNKIND WORDS.

THE words that thrilled with sweetest joy,
   We may sometimes forget.   In vain
We struggle to forget those words
   That pierced our hearts with pain.

ROSE OR THORN ?

[Quoted lines are from Harbaugh's " The Rose in the Heart."]

" THE roses of earth, let them wither and fade,
  And away in the shroudlets of winter be laid,
  For memory's fingers, unaided by art,
  Have planted a rose in the depth of the heart."

" It may be a love that was brief as a day,"
  Whose memory rises to madness! Ah, pray
  The kiss of forgetfulness, let it impart
  Sweet balm to the wounds of the thorn in the
      heart.

" It may be a song that has flitted away,"
  We hear the sweet echo, remember the lay,
  And treasure the voices that speak to impart
  New life to the withering rose in the heart.

" It may be a kiss—even kisses depart,"
  My God! dost Thou call this " the rose in the
      heart ? "

Ah, who would remember love's kisses now
    dead ?
The rose long has withered, the thorn lives
    instead.

" It may be a kiss "—oh, the depth of the pain
In the heart that remembers love's kisses in vain,
And memory, weeping, yet struggles to prove,
Though lost in the darkness, the dream was true
    love.

The springtime, the day of the roses—fair morn,
The autumn reveals the dead leaves and the thorn;
Sing memory's praises, yes, sing ye who will,
I 'd sleep in the arms of forgetfulness still.

THE CHILD AMONG THE FLOWERS.

Long ago, 't was in the springtime,
  I espied a child so sweet,
Kneeling like a little fairy
  'Mongst the flowers at his feet.
Long he sat there, seemed to listen
  To the voices glad and gay,
That were wafted from the flowers,
  To the child about his play.

And I listened, heard the baby
  Kiss the rose in tenderness,
Then I saw the bud unfolding,
  Him to bless with loveliness ;
Heard the prattling infant murmur,
  " Why art thou so sweet and fair,
Gentle blossom, that thy beauty
  Is remembered everywhere ? "

Said the rose, " My little lover,
  From the hand of God I came;
Should I die and be forgotten,
  I should cause my Maker shame.

87

You have eyes to see my beauty,
　　Ears have you to hear my voice;
If you 'd live and live forever,
　　Oh, be good, be glad, rejoice.

" If I heeded darkness dreary,
　　If I heard what people say,
I would droop and die, my lover,
　　All my sweet would pass away.
But I save my choicest perfume
　　For the kisses of the sun,
And he smiles upon me gently
　　All the day, my little one.

" Well I know if springtime showers,
　　Fall upon and wet my face,
He will kiss away my tear-drops,
　　And his touch my beauty grace.
When he hides from me I 'm sleepy
　　And I nod my pretty head,
If he leaves me long I slumber,
　　Then they tell you I am dead.

" Now so many things I 've told you,
　　Yet another word I 'd say,—

If you would be great and noble,
   Learn to love and learn to pray.
If your prayers and love are fruitful,
   You must noble be and great;
Seek the light and bathe in sunshine,
   This the key to golden gate.''

Then the whisper ceased, I listened,
   But the child made no reply;
Soon I heard the twilight echoes,
   Stars appeared within the sky.
I had been asleep, and dreaming,
   Had I sat for many hours,
When I found my baby sleeping
   'Mongst the fragrant, dreaming flowers.

I MISS YOU FROM OUR LITTLE
TRUNDLE-BED.

THEY have laid you, little brother,
   In a little casket white,
In a room so cold and silent,
   And I 'm all alone to-night.
Mamma knows I want you, brother,
   In our little trundle-bed,
Oh, I cannot sleep without you,
   And they tell me you are dead.

But I think you 're with the angels,
   Mamma says you 've gone to heav'n.
Do you miss me, little brother,
   'Mong the boys up there in heaven ?
Do they love you as I love you ?
   Can they see me when I cry ?
I don't know why they should leave me
   When they took you to the sky.

Oh, I wish that I could hear you
   When you sing up there to-night,

And could see you—mamma says you
  Wear a crown that 's shining bright.
If your soul is up in heaven,
  Then I 'm sure you are not dead;
But we 'll sleep no more together
  In our little trundle-bed.

I am thinking of last Christmas,
  How you called me in the night,
Whispered, " Brother, let us waken,
  If we can, before daylight."
When the morning came you wakened
  Just before I did, and said :
" Brother, see! our Christmas presents
  On our little trundle-bed."

And 't is Christmas in the morning,
  And I guess you 're glad in heaven,
Hope that Santa has forgotten,
  And no presents shall be given
Just to me, for there 's no pleasure
  In a story-book and sled,
For I 'll miss you in the morning
  From our little trundle-bed.

Just a week ago to-night, when
   We had knelt and said our prayers,
I remember how you whispered,
   " There are angels on the stairs."
And I cried, for I was frightened,
   But you held me close and tight,
Then I slept and dreamed of heaven,
   And the angels came that night.

When the morning came I missed you,
   Papa rocked you by the fire,
Mamma cried—we heard the angels
   Coming nigher, nigher, nigher.
Now you 're with them and I 'm lonely,
   But to-night our mamma said,
That you 'll come back with the angels
   To our little trundle-bed.

WHERE SONGS ABOUND.

In hearts where the sunlight scarce enters, where
    darkness
And sorrow and sadness and weeping are there,
Where poverty pinches, and kindness is wanting,
    The finger of God plants a song bright and
    fair.

The birth of the kind thought that yearned to be
    spoken,
    The tear-drop that fell in the dark of the night,
The hunger and thirst for the true light of
    heaven,
    Are poems of beauty, of sweetness and light.

And some sing their songs to the glad world, and
    others
    Sing low to a heart in its anguish and pain;
Some gather the roses that bloom in the garden,
    And some dare not pluck the wild rose of the
    plain.

But, O weary heart, do not faint — songs are sweetest
  When born at the breath of the wild winds, maybe,
The beautiful bird in a gold cage sings sweetly,
  Yet swift flies the bird of the wild prairie sea.

I know in each heart lies a gem of great beauty,
  The sweetest of songs have been sung all unheard,
And poems have lived in the heart where was hidden
  Forever in darkness each beautiful word.

I know that the light of a golden forever
  Shall burnish the gold that 's now hidden in dross;
I know there is joy beyond Time's darksome river,
  O patient one, weary one, cling to the Cross!

THE LAST WORDS OF MOTHER.

The last words of mother when I left the farm—
A bright, happy boy, never dreaming of harm—
She wept, and she left her sweet kiss on my face,
While looking to God, in the parting, for grace,
And then as I galloped away she called, " Roy,"
I turned in my saddle—" God bless you, my boy."

The years quickly vanished, I wandered afar,
Grew reckless and weary, it seemed every star
Was blotted from heaven, so dark was my night,
So cruel my fate, when, at last, shone a light
In the heart that sin's curse had long sought to
    destroy,—
The last words of mother, " God bless you, my
    boy."

The waves rolled between us, I ne'er saw her
    more,
And yet as I 'd done in the sweet days of yore,
I sat in the twilight and sang mother's songs,
And wept bitter tears o'er the past and its wrongs.

When others have cursed me these words gave me
    joy—
The last words of mother, " God bless you, my
    boy."

Methinks in the light of that beautiful home,
When toiling is over, no longer to roam,
The words that recalled me from sin and its charm,
When I went a-roaming and left the old farm,
When mother shall greet me, perchance, then in joy
She 'll murmur these loved words, " God bless you,
    my boy."

COULD YOU BUT KNOW.

Could you but know, my dearest one,
   I watch and wait for you,
When morning sunlight sheds its gleam,
   When evening skies are blue;
And could you know how faint my heart,
   How long and lone the day,
And how I prize your coming, dear,
   You would not stay away.

But time goes on, a year has flown,
   Yet hope, my guiding star,
Still counts the days through blinding tears,
   And calls you from afar.
Could you but know how true my heart,
   How firm my trust alway,
And how I love you, love you, dear,
   You would not stay away.

OUR BLESSINGS.

WHEN the morning sun in splendor
  Rises gently to its height,
And the beauty of the morning
  Giveth greeting after night;
While the bees are sipping honey
  From the early blooming flowers,
Then it is we count our blessings,
  Through the bright and happy hours.

Some have wealth, and golden roses
  Seem to bloom along their way;
Others wear the shining laurels
  Fame can give in life's short day.
Some have faces clothed in beauty,
  Some have lovers brave and true,
Some have friends that seem so many
  As the stars in heaven's blue.

All of these recount their blessings,
  While I kneel to God in prayer,

And I praise Him for the jewels
  He has trusted to my care.
I have naught of wealth or leisure,
  Though, perchance, I may have friends,
And methinks the smiles of angels
  On my home the Father sends.

When I see my first-born kneeling
  By his snowy cot to pray,
When the night shades hover o'er us
  At the closing of the day ;
When my little girl is singing
  Like the birds with song to bless,
And my baby's laugh is ringing,
  I have all of happiness.

Then there 's one—I 'd not forget him,
  With his eyes of tender blue—
Whispers, while I kiss his tresses,
  " Mamma, but I do love you."
While the days are going onward,
  Some may laugh and others pray,
But we all may count our blessings
  And rejoice the darkest day.

WHEN I SEE THE CHILDREN COMING HOME FROM SCHOOL.

When I see the children coming home from school,
Gaily singing when at last they 're free from rule,
    In their joy I have a share,
    For it rolls away my care,
Just to see the children coming home from school.

With their dinner-buckets swinging at their side,
Hear them shout as o'er the icy ground they glide;
    Home, they greet me with a kiss,
    And this thought is born in bliss,
To a mother, God no blessing has denied.

There 's a note of sadness in my song to-day,
For I 've seen beyond the present far away;
    Oh, my heart, how shall it be,
    When my children go from me ?
Will my heart ache ? yet they 've taught me how to
    pray.

When I see the children coming home from school,
I must wreathe my face in smiles, for 't is my rule
  To be happy, bright, and gay,
  Ere the dear ones go away,
And no more I see them coming home from school.

HER LAST FAREWELL.

My dear, I 've much to say to thee,
　Come sit thee by my bed
And gaze upon me, loved one—lay
　Thy hand upon my head;
And let thine eyes in tenderness,
　In gentle beauty shine
Upon my face, and do not heed
　The dimness now in mine.

The peaceful morning gives to me
　A spirit of unrest,
Oh, take me to thine arms, my dear,
　And fold me to thy breast.
The singing of the joyful birds
　Is very sad to me ;
To-morrow morning when they sing
　I shall have gone from thee.

The parting time has come, and I
　Have loved thee true and well,

And when I 'm gone thou 'lt sometimes come
   And wander in the dell
Where I 'm at rest, and kneel beside
   Me as I 'm sleeping there,
And promise thou wilt meet me in
   The home so bright and fair.

It seems again I 'm in the past,
   My love, I 'm at thy side—
A blushing girl—thy whispered words
   Have made of me thy bride.
And thou art smiling as in youth,
   Oh, thou art glad and gay,
The years that intervene since then
   Have vanished for to-day.

How cheerily we ventured out
   Upon the sea of life,
My hand in thine, my husband, and
   The name you called me—wife.
We planted flowers at the door
   Of our first humble home ;
I cannot say good-bye just now,
   In youth's glad days I roam.

Canst thou forget, my love, when first
    A tiny babe was given ?
Thy kisses rained upon my brow,
    And then I dreamed of heaven.
One morn when I was fast asleep,
    Thy hands placed on my breast
The first sweet flowers that bloomed for us,
    And now, when I 'm at rest

Again upon my bosom thou
    Wilt place the fragrant flowers,
And dream a little while, perchance,
    Of joys that have been ours.
Thou 'lt press thy warm, red lips to mine,
    I shall not know thy touch.
My God! this parting tells me that
    I 've loved thee overmuch.

And when they take me from thee, and
    They lay me 'neath the sod,
Don't think of me as lost to thee,
    But know that I 'm with God.
And oh, I plead, do not forget
    When trials pass thy way,

That with my latest breath for strength
　To conquer them I pray.

Press on, my dearest husband, just
　A little way beyond
Thou 'lt see the light of heaven that
　For me has almost dawned.
I 'm going—hold me closer—as
　I love thee none can tell;
Just one kiss more—God bless thee! meet
　Me over there—farewell.

LOVE'S DREAM.

As the flowers come in Springtime,
   Came love's dream to me, and light
As the touch of fairy fingers,
   Was love's step that starry night.
Long I revelled in the sunshine
   Of his bright, love-laden eyes,
Then my dream of love had vanished
   Like the jewels in the skies.

Is the dream in all its sweetness
   Ended, and for aye?—pray tell,
Ye who love and hope in heaven,
   Ye who say good-bye—ah, well,
This Old Time cannot take from me:
   Voices sweet and soft and low,
And the spirit form so near me,
   Breathes a prayer I fain would know.

He has held me to his bosom,
   I have felt his thrilling kiss,

And together in love's sweetness,
  We have melted into bliss.
We have parted, yet in seeming
  Would our spirits fan the blue,
In the poetry of loving,
  Knowing well each heart is true.

Tell me not love's dream is over,
  Can the bounding spirit feel?
See! the bar is in the fire,
  And the fire is in the steel.
So the heart is like a casket,
  He who placed a jewel there,
Will forget or be forgotten,
  Not while cloudless skies are fair.

TO A FRIEND.

You write sweet verses, I write verses, too;
  We ne'er have met, nor have you been a guest
  In homes where I am known.   Yet, dearest, best,
Of all my friends, my heart is holding you—
And why ?   How do I know your friendship true ?
  " Like partners in a dance," you said—the test
  Lies in those words, my friend—I leave the rest.
" Like partners in a dance," ah, then, we two,
As in a dizzy waltz, go on and on,
  Our steps the rhythm and our souls the rhyme.
What tho' you sing a song more glad, more sweet
Than any lay of mine ?   Perchance I 've drawn
  Some strains from out my lyre in truer time,
As in the dance, I lean on you—'t is meet.

I WANT TO BE GOOD.

" I WANT to be good," the little one said,
  As he nestled his head on his mother's breast.
And wept o'er the wee little sins of the day,
  " I want to be good," and he sank to rest.

" I want to be good," said a fair young girl
  Who had all of life's joys and none of its woes,
And with never a dream what the wish might mean,
  She pinned on her bosom a pure white rose.

" I want to be good," cried an aching heart,
  " But, oh, I 've no strength in the storms of life ;
I 've tried, I have struggled, and yet I have sinned,
  And my ship goes down 'mid the battle's strife."

Ah, list to the voice that speaks in each heart,
  In the heaven-kissed hours of solitude,
The life may be evil, and yet, maybe,
  Even so—to be good is the spirit's mood.

TWILIGHT MUSINGS.

SOMETIMES when day is done I love to sit
  And ponder o'er the past, and idly dream,
To listen to the spirit words that flit
  On wings of love thro' heart and brain, and seem
To give me back my olden joys—aye, more,
  They give me back myself as in the past,
My dearest self e'en as I was before
  I 'd " supped with sorrow "—would those dreams
    might last!

But, no, they tarry not with me, nor bless,
  Because they leave my heart so lone and sad,
They mock me with my vanished happiness,
  They fill with tears my eyes once bright and glad;
They wring my heart with longings for lost youth,
  Then thrill me with a touch almost divine,
They give me back my love, my grace, in truth
  Once more the thrill of passion's kiss is mine.

And then I consecrate, with newer zeal,
  To this the past, the radiant past, the hours

When love illumed the eye, the heart could feel
 The joyful carol of the birds; when flowers
Seemed not to die, so quick they bloomed anew.
 I give to thee, O golden past, my tears,
My memories, my fairer self, and true
 To those thou gavest me—all, all my years.

YOU WILL FORGET.

You will forget—ah, love, I surely know
This painful silence as love's deadliest foe;
   Not so with me—think you I could forget?
   This silence tears me, and my soul doth fret,
My longings drive me mad, e'en to bestow,
As in the past, one kiss, one whispered low
" I love you " ; but the years will come and go,
   And I shall bless the hour in which we met—
      You will forget.

I do not blame, I know it must be so;
I loved thee well, with thee 't was passion's glow.
   Ofttimes when all alone my lids are wet,
   Oh, just to be remembered, love, and yet
I shall remember and be true—I know
      You will forget.

SYMPATHY.

I WENT to the house of mourning,
  And knelt with the mourners in prayer,
And all thro' the house there was weeping,
  So tender were all who were there.
And I thought how the blessed Redeemer
  Took note of each tear-drop that fell,
And I knew if my own home were saddened,
  I, too, would be mourned long and well.

But standing apart from the others
  Was one who had sorrow so deep,
That almost she envied the dear one
  Who lay in such peace there asleep.
And I waited—no word said to cheer her,
  Tho' she 'd borne her great burden for years,
Not a tear shed for her—all were weeping,
  And, perchance, saw her not for their tears.

ONLY BE TRUE.

FRIEND, thou art tempted and weary,
   Yet in the conflict, I pray,
Hope in her arms shall enfold thee,
   Love, faith, and trust bide the day.
E'en now 't is dawn of the morning,
   Light gleams across heaven's blue,
Fling to the breeze the white banner,
   Weary one, only be true.

True to the best that is in thee,
   True to the right, friend, alway,
So shalt thou drink drops of mercy—
   Heavenly nectar—yet stay,
Hear me once more, I entreat thee,
   Ere I shall bid thee adieu;
Look whence the morning light cometh,
   Look, and forever be true.

MY FRIENDS.

THE world is like a cold midwinter day,
 And in it, like the beggar at the door,
Ofttimes with hungry hearts we turn away,
 For there is no admittance. Yet before
 We turn to go, hope bids us knock once more,
The cold winds pierce our frame—we wait, our
   prayers
Are all unheard—alas, nobody cares.

I 've read a book—you 've read it, too, I ween,
 And you, like me, sat poring o'er the tale
And weeping. Yet, a sadder thing I 've seen—
 A slowly breaking heart, a face grown pale—
 I guess the secret pain, and yet I fail
In sympathy, the thing is all too real.
I wonder what it is we mortals feel ?

And so I value not the world's applause,
 To-day 't would bless, to-morrow let me die;
And yet I love to plead true friendship's cause,
 I 'd wave her starry banners to the sky—
 No warmer heart hast thou, my friend, than I—
And into faithful lives the Father sends,
With all things needful, good and honest friends.

FRIENDSHIP ONLY.

YES, we are only friends, but dear the tie
　　That binds our very souls; and it is best
　　For you, my friend, and best for me to rest
In this sweet peace, nor wake at last to sigh
　　For sweeter chords to bind our hearts in one—
A closer tie—ah, dear, the hope is vain,
Your path lies yonder, mine is here.　In vain
　　And sore at heart, we'd wish the chords undone.

I know your heart could answer mine; I own
　　The sweet response that echoes in my soul,
　　And oft I would that I might give the whole
Of this great throbbing heart to you alone.
　　I know your kiss would wake the sleeping fires
That in my bosom burn, but then, I say,
'T is best for you and best for me alway,
　　To be as friends—friendship hath no desires.

A REVERIE.

ALMOST the time has come for us to part—
Myself and my blest Youth—and in my heart
A secret pain lies hidden, for I know
'T is vain to cling, as well to bid her go;
And yet I hold her fast, so fast in dread
Of waking from my dreams to find her fled.
Thus far we 've walked together hand in hand,
So kind, so gentle, can she understand
That one so fair must dwell among the flowers,
While I go forth to wrestle weary hours,
Yea, weary years instead, where darkness dwells?
Her laughing eyes, her smiling face foretells
She knows it not.   And yet I know it well
That soon Old Time shall ring the passing-bell,
And Youth and I will part—she will not die,
But leave me, leave me! oh, I 'll say good-by,
And face the storms she will not brave with me,
And struggle to forget.   But then, maybe,
When I have learned contentment at the last,
I 'll hear her voice as in the dear, sweet past;

It may be she will waft to me a kiss,
Remembering the past and all its bliss.
And then together for the happy time,
Our steps in rhythm and our souls in rhyme,
We 'll wander forth once more, forgetting all,
How I am bent and gray, she young and small
Like fairy elf; and yet, my God! to-day
I hold her fast—my hair it is not gray,
My eyes still hold their light, my heart is warm,
How can I kiss her lips and face the storm,
And know that we no more shall meet ?—stay, stay,
Fair Youth, oh, leave me not, I plead, I pray—
My God! the hour has come, and we must part!
So soon ?   Yes, yes; it tears my heart!
Come, glue thy lips to mine, sweet one; in truth
I 'd give my life to spare thee this, O Youth.

MY TRUST.

I KNELT alone with God one day,
   I felt my heart at once rebel,
Oh, could I trust and could I pray,
   When first I must repent ?   I fell
From heaven to a demon's hell
   While there I struggled, yet I must
Tear from my heart my idol—well,
   I seemed to hear a voice say, " Trust."

Dost Thou require me, Lord, to lay
   Upon Thine altar all ?   Oh, tell
Me not this is Thy will—nay, nay,
   For want of courage do I sell
My soul to darkness ?—break this spell
   That holds my heart in evil!   Dost
Thou pity when sin hath befell ?
   I seemed to hear a voice say, " Trust."

Then all at once, I cannot say
   What 't was that seemed my doubts to quell.

I yielded all my soul, that day
  Low at the feet of Christ I fell,
And knew that I was blest!   " Farewell,"
  I cried, and saw my idols dust,
And as was rung the passing-bell,
  I seemed to hear a voice say, " Trust."

ENVOY.

Blest Saviour, let me only dwell
  Where I may hear Thy voice.   And dost
Thou save me from my sins ?—'t is well,
  I seemed to hear a voice say, " Trust."

THAT SWEET, SAD WAY.

I HAVE noticed that love hath changeful ways,
  Sometimes she is on the wing,
And happy as birds on summer days,
  She can only laugh and sing.
But then it is true, though the skies are blue,
  And love revels in delight,
In the gladsome song some discords rise,
  Like clouds on a starlit night.

For life is night and love the stars
  That gladden our darkened sky,
And even a note of joy oft mars
  A dream that awakes to die.
Then gentle and sweet, it is ever meet
  That love should be glad and gay,
But passion as deep as the ocean's depth,
  I see in that sweet, sad way.

The bright eyes soft with the unshed tears,
  And the voice so kind and low,

'T is a love that is free from doubts and fears,
  'T is a gift from God, we know.
And my heart is glad, and my heart is sad,
  And I sing and then I pray,
Whenever the one I love is near,
  And wearing that sweet, sad way.

I THINK OF THEE.

I THINK of thee, my own, my dear,
My heart is glad, my song is clear
  As fairy songs that wing their flight
  To mystic vales all clothed in light;
And when I dream, thou art so near,
And yet so far; I seem to hear
Thy tender voice, thy words of cheer,
    One face doth each fair dream bedight,
      I think of thee.

I sweetly dream and know no fear,
No demon forms shall dare appear,
  To wrest from me those visions bright,
  Those stolen kisses—what delight!
Let daylight fade, is darkness drear?
    I think of thee.

TO IRENE.

Ofttimes I wonder, lady-bird, Irene,
  Dost thou remember still that summer day
  When first we met ?   Ah, yes, I think alway
Thy heart will faithful be.   My gentle queen,
E'en from that day thy face no more I 've seen,
  Yet in that hour ye stole my heart away,
  And thinkest thou, Irene, my thought could stray?
Could oil or water, dear one, come between
  Our welded souls ?   Ah, no! and thou art mine!
    And in the precious locket of our hearts
Our secret hopes lie hidden—yet, I ween,
  E'en tho' the love-light in thine eye doth shine,
    At thought of all our loneliness oft starts
The bitter tear—is 't so, my sweet Irene ?

TO-NIGHT.

I 'm tired to-night,
　　So sing me soft and low
Some plaintive little song
　　Of long ago.

Or read to me
　　From out the Book of Life,
That I may find new grace
　　For daily strife.

To-night I would
　　That I could put away
Those memories so dear,
　　Content to pray.

UNDER THE SMILE.

You look on my face, I am smiling,
    You enter my home, it is fair,
And you say that the gods are beguiling
    My moments to happiness there.
Then you kiss me, oh, sweetly and tender,
    And your kiss may be free from art,
But you heard not amid this splendor
    The wail of my breaking heart.

Into homes where the traces of hunger
    On dear little faces I see,
I go when the twilight is longer,
    To carry sweet roses, may be.
And almost do those mothers despise me,
    They envy my happier part,
And almost do I fail to disguise me,
    Almost would I show them my heart.

There are mothers in plain muslin dresses,
    More blest than was ever a queen,

And they finger the fair golden tresses
   Of little ones, this I have seen.
In her ermine and delicate laces,
   A woman bent low 'neath the smart
Of pain, while she hid from all faces
   The tale of the woe in her heart.

So I laugh and I sing, and in seeming,
   I 'm gay, and the world may go by,
What matter while others are dreaming,
   If some in the cold grave would lie ?
We kiss when we greet one another,
   " God bless you," we say, and depart,
While we pray God to grant we may smother
   The wail of a broken heart.

IF I WRITE.

If I write the noblest essays
  That have bless'd the hearts of men ;
If I consecrate my whole life
  To the mission of my pen,
I can yet improve my writings,
  I can tear up or erase,
I can blot out, interline it,
  And for losses add new grace.

If I chisel in the marble
  With a firm and skilful hand,
If I wish my work for ages
  To be praised o'er all the land;
If, perchance, I might deface it,
  Though I toiled with earnest care,
I can carve the work all over,
  I have marble I can spare.

If I teach a noble lesson
  To a precious little child,

I have written it forever,
  Though he pass through storms most wild.
God has made my work immortal,
  I have cut it not in stone,
But in heart of flesh I wrote it,
  Work that God delights to own.

Ah, I 'd love to be a writer,
  I would love to wear Fame's crown,
I would love to hear the echo
  Of the far-off world's renown,
But, O Father, I would ask Thee
  If to write I am beguiled,
Let me do my noblest writing
  On the heart of someone's child.

THE WHISTLING BOY.

My neighbor's boy, shoes out at toes,
    Is of all boys most truly blest ;
He heeds not though the north wind blows,
    This boy who seeks not ease and rest;
And oft I 've to my heart confessed,
    Though whistling may some souls annoy,
I would not have one note suppressed—
    How well I love thee, whistling boy !

He gaily whistles, yet, who knows
    If 'neath that ragged coat that breast
Is burdened with the weight of woes,
    When daylight darkens in the west ?
For, oh, within that boy's home nest
    Is sorrow, want, and little joy,
Yet still he whistles—hast thou guessed
    How well I love thee, whistling boy ?

We all may learn to speak in prose,
    And can but make a rhyme at best ;

O'er weary hearts we plant a rose,
   And call on angels to attest.
But who like thee, my little guest,
   So brave, so happy, and so coy,
Can whistle at the soul's behest ?
   How well I love thee, whistling boy !

Methinks if angels went in quest
   Of whistling boys, they 'd thee employ.
All hearts with joy thou dost revest,
   How well I love thee, whistling boy!

SLEEP SWEETLY.

SLEEP sweetly, O my little one,
　　I leave thee to the night,
And pray that angels from afar,
　　Thy dreaming thoughts bedight.

Sleep on, sleep on, nor wake to weep,
　　That we shall meet no more;
The angels even now are come,
　　Are knocking at the door.

My little one, my darling one,
　　I go to be at rest,
While thou art sweetly dreaming in
　　My arms.　Ah, if 't were best,

I would thine eyes might just unclose
　　One moment ere I go,
To bless me with the baby love,
　　That 's written there I know.

But sleep on now, my little one,
　　I 'll go ere dawns the light
Of 'morrow's sun.　God keep my child—
　　One kiss—good-night, good-night.

APART.

THERE may be those who can forget,
　　There may be those whose love can die,
And other loves prove sweet—and yet,
　　As day by day goes by,
I dream of him in distant lands,
　　Whose voice I ne'er shall hear again,
Nor feel the touch of his dear hands,
　　Nor wake from tears and pain.

But this I know, through all the years
　　That are to come I 'll love but one;
For him my tenderness, my tears,
　　Until life's race is run.
He heard and heeded duty's call,
　　And, oh, amid the cold world's snares,
I sent him forth and gave him all—
　　My love, my faith, my prayers.

We 'll meet no more; my heart is dumb,
　　And yet it seems this cannot be;

But then if I should bid him come,
   Resigning all for me,
My kiss would sting him at the last,
   He 'd rend the chains he fain would wear,
No, no! our hopes, our dreams—the past—
   Are voices stilled in prayer.

IN WOMAN'S WORLD.

In woman's world do song-birds sing
Throughout the year ?   Does gladness ring
   From dawn till dark her golden bell,
   In woman's world ?   Ah, who can tell ?
But, ah, methinks, on silvery wing
Heaven's echoes come like birds in spring,
'Round woman's throne all clustering;
   And we are told 't is blest to dwell
      In woman's world.

If thou art worn and wandering
In paths of sin and suffering,
   And fain would drink from mercy's well,
   Come hither, come beneath love's spell,
For sweet love is the offering
      In woman's world.

HAVE FAITH IN GOD.

Upon the air a voice is borne
    That 's heard o'er land and sea,
Its music charms the dreary land,
    It lulls to sleep the sea.
It sings around the stars above,
    It whispers 'neath the sod,
The words of cheer it speaks to all
    Are these, " Have faith in God."

One day while singing glad and gay,
    A moan it chanced to hear,
It came from one of broken heart
    Within a hovel near.
A little form in robes of white
    Was sleeping 'neath the sod;
The voice said, " Thou shall see the child
    Again.   Have faith in God."

" Have faith in God," so said the voice
    One dismal wintry day,

When orphaned children, one, two, three,
  Had knelt for bread to pray.
No need had they, the tender lambs,
  To feel the chastening rod,
And ere the prayer was finished they
  Had food.   Have faith in God.

Drinking the bitter dregs of sin,
  A man and wife must part,
While weeping children cling to each,
  And heart is torn from heart.
" Alas! " cried they, " there is no hope
  Until beneath the sod
We shall forget " ; but hear the voice
  Sing out, " Have faith in God."

And can it be that faith in God
  Can make the bitter sweet ?
Can mend the broken, right the wrong ?
  Then kneel at Jesus' feet.
Who needs must sink in dark despair
  Beneath the chastening rod ?
There is no wrong God cannot right,
  Look up!   Have faith in God.

Then blessed be the happy voice,
   That sings o'er land and sea,
And ever says, " Have faith in God;
   His love shall make thee free."
Sing on, sweet voice, we 've heard thee oft
   Where aching feet have trod,
And, oh, we welcome thee alway,
   Sing on, " Have faith in God."

And so upon its mission glad,
   It breathes upon the air
Forever gentle words of love,
   To save men from despair.
If thou art sinking 'cause of pain
   Beneath the chastening rod,
Ah, kiss the rod, 't is sent in love;
   Sing on—Have faith in God.

PRAYER.

FATHER, I cannot speak the words
   My heart so yearns to say;
The night is lone and dark and drear,
   And gloom enshrouds my way.
And Thou canst see the spectral forms
   That rise up in the night
And beckon me.   I plead, I pray,
   Lead me, oh, lead aright.

I cannot tell where Thou shalt lead,
   Thou knowest; I but ask
Prepare my life, my heart, my hands
   To do each tiny task.
And teach me, Lord, to do Thy will,
   On Thee to cast my care,
And teach me how to pray—perchance
   Obedience is prayer.

DEAR ONE, ADIEU.

God bless thee, dear, and now good-bye;
The sun sinks low in yonder sky,
Then haste away, nor think of me,
Though my heart break and bleed for thee.
Where duty calls I bid thee go,
Be brave, be hopeful, dear, and know
As long as cloudless skies are blue,
I love but thee, I will be true.

Where duty calls I see afar,
The blazing gleam of fame's bright star,
And bid thee go; I can but stay
And love thee well, and for thee pray.
Not mine to comprehend thy task,
We part forever—I but ask,
When days are dark and friends are few,
Remember, then, I will be true.

Some day on other lips shall burn
Those kisses, passion born—yet turn

From me away and seek the one
Whose mate thou art; ah, then, well done
Shall be my life work when I know
That I have aided thee.   Ah, go,
And climb the heights; dear one, adieu,
One farewell kiss—I will be true.

WE 'LL MEET AGAIN.

We 'll meet again, my heart doth say,
And this my hope from day to day;
   It cannot be that cruel fate
   Hath shut and barred love's golden gate,
And thou hast all forgotten; nay,
I trust thee more. Some gentle fay
Keeps singing to my heart alway,
   And oft doth she asseverate,
      We 'll meet again.

Life is the stage, our love the play,
The curtain has gone down,—yet stay,
   Can aught true love obliterate ?
   Some fair, sweet day, if soon or late,
In love's own way, my heart doth say,
      We 'll meet again.

I 'M WAITING FOR YOU.

The night shades are falling,
  The sunlight has fled,
The lamps are now lighted,
  The table is spread.
I stand in the twilight,
  I 'm kissed by the dew,
While watching, dear papa,
  And waiting for you.

I 'm waiting for you with
  A kiss, papa dear,
I 've roses to give you,
  And sunshine and cheer.
The bright stars are peeping
  From out heaven's blue,
Come quickly, dear papa,
  I 'm waiting for you.

LEAD THEM HOME.

I COULD tell of days made happy
    By a husband's tender kiss,
Of a home of love and beauty,
    Of a fairer day than this.
When the night winds ne'er would whisper
    Such a tale as now they tell,
Since the years have flown, and lonely
    Is my heart and home—ah, well,

I remember how my husband,
    When the evening lights were lit,
Used to love to sit beside me,
    And to watch me sing and knit,
While our little ones were dreaming,
    And our hearts were young and gay;
But 't was in the past, my gladness,
    And I 'm all alone to-day.

For the " little ones " have wandered
    Out upon the sea of life,

Twenty years ago my husband
  Whispered, '' Meet me there, sweet wife.''
Twenty years,—a long, long waiting,—
  But the meeting time is near,
I am old and bent and wrinkled,
  And my sight no longer clear.

'' Over there '' is home so precious,
  Home for children and for me,
Home where husband waits and watches
  For our coming.   Seems I see
Once again each dear one climbing
  Into father's old armchair,
While he smiles and rocks the babies,
  In the home once bright and fair.

And the children ne'er shall gather
  In our earthly home again,
Ere they come again to mother,
  She 'll have passed from toil and pain.
O my Father, do Thou hear me,
  Guide the children lest they roam,
Over life's tempestuous ocean,
  Father, safely lead them home.

THE PARTING.

In long years of weeping,—
   Is 't sin ?—God forbid!—
My heart still is keeping
   Our secret close hid.

I 've known little pleasure,
   Yet after the showers
The sunshine we treasure,—
   I 've known some bright hours.

And yet, 't is our duty
   Forever to part;
For us there 's no beauty
   In heaven, sweetheart,

Unless, in that fair home
   Where weary ones rest,
E'en as now, thou mayest come
   And rest on my breast;

Unless, e'en as now, dear,
   I thrill 'neath thy kiss,
I cannot allow, dear,
   In heaven there 's bliss.

My God! I 'll regret thee,
   Too sweet was our love ;
Think not I 'll repent me,
   More faithful I 'll prove.

Shall memory haunt me ?
   God pity me, then,
Thy kisses will taunt me,—
   We 'll ne'er meet again.

We part, and forever,
   Yet fond hearts and true
No partings can sever,—
   O sweet one, adieu.

SHOW THE WORLD WHAT YOU CAN DO.

I 'm a fool that I don't do it!—
  Send a bullet through my brain,
I have lost my all forever,
  Life is loss and death were gain.
In this lonely, dreary dungeon,
  Weeping tears of shame alone,
Friends I 've loved and that have loved me,
  Pass me by as though unknown.

And my wife yearns to forget me,
  While my baby calls in vain,
Seems I hear the child say, " Mamma,
  Will papa come home again ? "
Oh, I 'm lost, I 'm wrecked, I 'm ruined,
  All my life my sin I 'll rue,
What is this that seems to whisper,
  " Show the world what you can do " ?

Show the world ! Ah! men would curse me
  If I held to them the stars,

If I gave them gold for ashes—
  I have been behind the bars.
But I 'll try; yes, I will do it,
  Rise above the world's disdain,
I will teach my wife to trust me,
  She shall kiss my lips again.

For to-night within my prison,
  Streaming through the cruel bars,
Comes the light God gives so gently,
  From His own, the countless stars.
Gazing upward, mercy whispers,
  Gently, sweetly, " God is true,
Loves thee ever, falters never,—
  Show the world what you can do."

Whence it came, this hopeful message,
  Whither gone, I know not where,
But I know that since its coming,
  It has chased away despair.
And I live to lose my sorrow
  In a life that 's brave and true,
In my heart this cherished motto:
  " Show the world what you can do."

MY VERSES AND MY FRIEND.

When first you read my verses,
  You thought them very good,
And I rejoiced—you know it—
  As but their author could.
But later, you re-read them,
  You find them faulty now—
You laugh because there lingers
  A cloud upon my brow.

When first, my friend, you loved me,
  You thought me only fair,
You told me I had beauty,
  You kissed my sunny hair.
We walked a pace together
  Then learned to disagree,
For now you know me faulty,
  No longer fair to thee.

When last you read my verses,—
  Pronounced them faulty,—then

I looked upon them only
  As scratches from a pen.
But in my heart they echo,
  Their birth was but a thrill
Of bygone joys remembered,
  I can but love them still.

And so, my friend, I pray you
  If faults you find in me,
Still love me and forgive me,
  And let us happy be.
Believe my heart is faithful,
  Though dark or light the sky,
And we shall still be happy
  Together—you and I.

I KNOW ONE HEART IS TRUE.

WE parted, and forever,
  O God! that last adieu,
'T would break my heart if not for this—
  I know one heart is true.

He 'll roam the wide world over,
  And love his path will strew
With sweet enticements, yet I know—
  I know one heart is true.

What though the days are dreary,
  Some penance must be due
For love so great—I am content—
  I know one heart is true.

Ah, true, yes true as heaven,
  And faithful hearts are few;
How sweet my rest, how firm my trust,
  I know one heart is true.

We ne'er shall meet again, love,
   The past we 'll not renew,
Yet each may say, and rightly, dear,
   " I know one heart is true."

You kissed my lips, and weeping
   We spoke the last adieu;
Until we meet in heaven at last,
   I know thou wilt be true.

LOVE'S RESPONSE TO LOVE.

YES, love, my heart responds
    With precious tribute due,
When thou dost say to me,
    " I know one heart is true."

Love answers back to love,
    As azure sky to blue,
As " deep to deep " the sea,
    Because two hearts are true.

The love I bear to thee
    Is kindled thus anew,
For " love is fed with love,"
    My dear, if love be true.

Sweet peace to thee, dear one,
    The goal of life pursue,
At quicker pace go on,
    Thy lover's love is true.

THE HIDDEN TREASURE.

O Love, like the waves of the ocean,
  So beautiful, boundless, and free,
Come hither, my heart, in its yearning,
  At rest on thy bosom would be.
I hold out my hands in entreaty,
  I plead that thy kiss may be mine,—
O Love, art thou deaf to my calling?
  My heart yields her treasure for thine.

I gaze on the night, and she whispers,
  " At twilight come hither, and Love,
Entreated, may lend his embraces."
  I gaze on the bright stars above;
The heavens are singing their love song,
  The earth in its darkness is drear,
At twilight I seek for my treasure,
  But find that it nowhere is near.

I turn to the morn in her glory,
  I see that the sun gives a kiss

To each humble rose, and the dew-drops
　　Are making bright eyes in their bliss.
And yet in their midst I 'm bewildered,
　　The treasure I seek cannot see,
I know not the way of enchantment,
　　And Love hies away, lost to me.

But now is my heart swept and garnished,
　　And bended my knees are in prayer;
Come hither, O Love, in thy fulness,
　　Nor doom me to death and despair.
I wait in my heart's deep contrition,
　　I yearn for thy kiss on my brow,
O God, Thou hast heard my petition,
　　And, Love, thou art blessing me now.

REMEMBRANCE.

Dost thou remember where we passed
  The sweet tuberoses in our stroll ?
Thou gavest me one rose, my friend,
  And in the garden of my soul
I hid it with the dream of joy
  The day had given—'t will impart
While life shall last, till dreams are past,
  A perfume rare from out my heart.

And oft as I remember now
  The beauty of the sun-kissed flowers,
The music of thy voice, my friend,
  The sweetness of those summer hours,
My soul pays tribute to the joys
  That memory can still impart,
From every searching eye is hid
  The happy past within my heart.

THE MYSTERY OF LOVE.

I.

BUT once to every soul King Love appears;
But once we bathe his feet with sacred tears;
We 've many a passion, many a dream of joy,
Full many a tender thought, but sweetly coy
The heart still slumbers till that summer noon
That smiles on every life, if late or soon,—
That golden hour when Nature lies in bloom,
All things beneath the sun new life assume,
And Love comes dressed in immortality,
And out we sail upon a golden sea.
Some souls there be who know him by his smile;
Still others know him not until, the while
He bends above them, on their thirsty lips
He drops a burning tear. One dear heart sips
The sweets of passion, and is well content;
Another seeking sympathy is bent.
And it may be King Love, his cause to plead,
Has but to search each heart and know its need.

II.

Since men have died for love, I 've tried, you 'll see,
To rend the veil that hides the mystery.
Is 't true that love is blind ?   They say 't is so!
Is love immortal ?   Ah, who this can know ?
Yet 't is not love, but passion mean and vile,
If aught can from its course true love beguile.
And did our God create two souls to mate ?
Then why, oh why, the cruelty of fate ?
Does love in turn beget love ?   Some have said;
But then, we know, not so the tale is read.
One gives his treasures all, and for his fee
Gets pain, or worse—indifference, may be;
A woman gives her soul!   Perchance, in turn
Receives a wound that evermore shall burn.
And few there be who all the journey long
Have tuned their lyres to sing love's perfect song.

III.

King Love forever will elude the grasp
Of lofty souls, who, seeking him, oft clasp
A thing that may his shadow prove; and then,
King Love himself (the silliness of men)

Will lose his head if beauty pass his way,
Tho' all the soul's delight he miss alway.
But wait; I think I said Love comes to all,
If soon or late, he comes to great and small.
Yet, see! he ofttimes enters where the gloom
Foretells the darkness of the waiting tomb;
On eyes grown blind with age he leaves a kiss,
And who can tell the mystery of this ?
Sometimes a fair young wife must be his prey,
He spares not any who may chance his way.
And then he comes with all enticements sweet,
When fettered are his hands and are his feet;
Ah, yes, he comes!—a most unwelcome guest
To many a heart, a stab to many a breast!
" Too late, too late! " o'er all the earth the cry;
" Too late, too late! King Love is passing by."
And yet, where is the heart that does not keep
The memory of his coming hidden deep
Amongst the fairest treasures of the soul ?
All hearts beat wild in blissful uncontrol
If on a summer noon he comes, and then
Thro' all the earth resounds one great Amen!
The flowers of heaven all bloom; in that glad hour
Drop fragrance like a sunlit summer shower.
But if King Love delay his coming long,

Methinks a hush falls over heaven's throng,
And angels say, " Impute it not as sin
If at his coming that heart let him in."
For " God is Love," and love He gives His own,
And by this grace alone shall they be known.
If Love comes late, 't is that His child may rest
In waiting on a loving Father's breast.
So if you think my story is confused,
'T is plain to Love's strange ways you are unused.

IV.

I 've sought out and can tell all things save this:
(And here my reasonings all go amiss)
Why is the heart condemned to still love on
When all the sweets of love fade and are gone ?
When Love himself hath pierced her thro' and
       thro'—
The lover changed—why cannot love change, too ?
Ah, this thing hath no soul the power to tell,
Love must be faithful to the last—'t is well;
And so, until we tread the streets above,
Man may not solve the mystery of love.

ONE LITTLE SWEET BLOSSOM.

One little sweet blossom, heav'n gave it to me,
So dainty and white, and the name—purity;
It was all that I owned, and I pined for the flowers
That bloomed in life's passionate sunnier hours.

One little sweet blossom, I put it aside,
Sailed out on the ocean of life deep and wide;
I bought and I treasured magnificent bloom,
I sought my fair treasures in sunshine and gloom.

I thirsted to gather the roses of fame,
I loved not my life, but an undying name;
I plucked the bright roses, but let fall the prize,
The little sweet blossom, my gift from the skies.

The pure heart and tender was folded in care,
My flowers all withered and died unaware;
Would I could exchange this great armful of flowers
For the little sweet blossom I held in youth's hours.

REMORSE.

I WRONGED thee—ah, 't is bitter now,
  Forgive, or yet forgive me not,
Whiche'er it be, thou wilt allow
  The deed can never be forgot.

I did thee harm.   O injured one,
  What I have felt thou hast not known;
I would recall the deed—'t is done!
  I suffer!   God, may this atone!

THINKING OF ME.

Thinking of me when you kneel to pray ?
Are you thinking of me this Sabbath day ?
  Does the peal of the joyful bells bring near
  The one to your heart most loved, most dear ?

I ofttimes wonder when far away,
When friends are near who are glad and gay,
If ever anon your thought will stray,
  And your heart find sweetest hope and cheer
      Thinking of me.

You have deemed me fair in your dreams—yet, stay!
It is not for this I would plead and pray;
  This—this, I ask, that your listening ear
  The words that my heart would speak may hear,
For you are, I know, this Sabbath day
      Thinking of me.

ETERNITY.

WHEN loved ones pass away we call it death;
We call it death, this passing of the breath,
This sleep that wraps the body in sweet rest,
And frees the soul to slumber on God's breast.
> We are so blind we fail to see
> Into the great eternity.

It is not death, this going on before,
And oft I fain would give the battle o'er;
Like loved ones that are gone, I, too, would sleep—
Sweet peace, sweet rest—the angels vigil keep
> The while we slumber, soon to be
> The children of eternity.

Each struggle that died out in weakness here,
When we have entered there it will appear
That angel hands have made the work complete,
To lay it as a trophy at our feet.
> For what we 've tried to do will be
> ·Rewarded in eternity.

The invalid that could not leave his chair,
To sip from Nature's fountain rich and rare,
The hand that, palsied, could not hold a flower,
Shall grasp immortal roses in that hour
>   When souls now fettered shall be free,
>   Time past, and dawns eternity.

The soul must be prepared to enter there;
I would not fail in this, or dark or fair,
Or rough or flower-strewn my way, at last
I 'd glide into the harbor, sails full mast,
>   To sail for aye that golden sea,
>   Eternity, eternity!

WOULD I WERE A BEE.

I 've watched the bee at work, at play,
   The lips of every flower
He tastes, and to those loved the best
   He clings thro' many an hour.

With one and all a welcome guest,
   Oh, sweet his scented bower,—
Dear heart, I would I were a bee,
   And you my choicest flower.

LOVE IS TRUE TO LOVE.

Dost ask if I 'll be true to thee—
  To thee, the one I love?
Go seek an answer in the works
  Of Him who rules above,
For all the works of Nature prove
  That love is true to love.

The flowers love the summer time;
  When springtime doth appear
The roses bloom in greeting, and
  In love to summer's cheer;
They love no other season, and
  They bloom but once a year.

The tiny little birdies do
  Rest safely in their nest;
The parent bird will seek them food
  Before he seeketh rest.
But why not feed the neighbor birds?
  He loves his own the best.

A mother loves her little one,
  And from him would she stray
To seek another child to love,
  Altho' it be more gay ?
Ah, love is ever true to love,
  And true love cannot stray.

The world is full of sinning ones
  Who reap as they have sown,
We pity them, for well we know
  Not true love have they known.
For set apart to purity
  Is she who wears love's crown.

WHEN YOU WENT AWAY.

I COULD not weep, and my heart stood still,
    That dismal day when you went away,
A hush o'er the household fell, until
    We spoke in a whisper all that day.

On the day you came, quite sure I am,
    There never were hearts so glad and gay,
I cried and I kissed your telegram—
    A treasure after you went away.

When you came your kiss was joyous, glad,
    And my heart sang out like birds in May,
But, oh, I would that your lips ne'er had
    Sought mine when I knew you going away.

Going away, and perhaps no more—
    Aye, never again on mine to rest
Those lips!—that is why that last kiss tore
    My heart from its moorings in my breast.

YOUR HEART.

You 've loved so many, yet your heart has some-
    thing new,
  Some treasure ne'er discovered by the seekers
    bold;
Perchance a rose, a lily white, a violet blue,
  That ne'er has bloomed—and it shall at my touch
    unfold.

COME BACK TO MY HEART.

Come back to my heart, my dear lost friend,
  Wait not to be welcomed there,
For the door 's ajar—thou art gone, and yet,
  Was thy home in my heart not fair ?
And there for thee do the roses bloom—
  Shall I see thy face no more,
Nor hear thy voice, though I love thee, dear,
  As in sweet, sweet days of yore ?

If the fault were mine, or if 't were thine,
  Let us, dear, forget, forgive;
And to each we 'll speak gentle words—oh, pray
  That the dear old friendship live.
Murmur, " Peace, be still ! " to the troubled heart
  Give again the old-time kiss,
Then we 'll wipe the tears from each other's eyes,
  On a fairer day than this.

Yes, dear, come back to my heart and rest ;—
  Oh, the day is lone and long,

And I guard the buds that shall bloom for thee
  When thou comest; and the song
Thou hast loved the best I shall sing no more
  Till I sing it to thine ear,
For I love thee still, oh, I love thee well—
  Come back to my heart, my dear.

SHE ONCE WAS FAIR.

SHE once was fair, I hear you say;
Her golden hair and eyes of gray
   Made in each heart for her a place,
   And that her sweet and gentle face
Was bright as noontide of the day;
You envied her, forgot to pray,
Because she chanced to pass your way,—
   Why say you then with laughing grace,
      She once was fair ?

When I am old, have lost each ray
Of beauty's light, oh, sing no lay
   Of sad regret; let time efface
   All that is fair, and weave her lace
Upon my brow—but do not say,
      She once was fair.

YE WELCOME DREAMS.

Ye welcome dreams, ye friends of night,
Born in the far-off realms of light,
  Come hither now, canst thou not spy
  The dark of night 'twixt earth and sky ?
Come and my fancies weave aright,
And lend me visions fair and bright;
Oh, let no evil omen 'fright
  Thy soft approach; I pray draw nigh,
    Ye welcome dreams.

In thine embrace, oh, what delight!
Ye bring me beauty, wealth and might,
  And love and wisdom from on high ;
  I 'd bid thee stay, nor say good-bye,
Yet morning dawns—good-night, good-night,
    Ye welcome dreams.

I WAS UNKIND.

I was unkind, and yet I knew
I loved him—then was love untrue ?
  Ah, me, I saw him turn away,
  He tried to smile, tried to be gay,
A pained look in his eyes of blue.
He knew not why as moments flew,
I silent was—an effort, too,
    It cost me, yet that fateful day
      I was unkind.

To-day were glad could I undo
The evil done; I would renew
  The happiness I wrecked, and say,
  " Forgive, oh, love, forgive, I pray ;
Look in my eyes—forget, will you ?
    I was unkind."

THE SUMMER IS GONE.

I KNEW not when she came what wealth of flowers
She 'd scatter 'neath my feet; nor did I know
From out her springs of joy there 'd come to flow
A river grand and deep.   Ah, golden hours,
Ye came to me in shady nooks and bowers,
So filled with happy voices soft and low,
I can but drop a tear.   As melts the snow,
As quickly come and go the springtime showers,
Ye vanished and are gone; but sweeter dreams
Than e'er I knew, and moments rich and rare,
Are hiding in my soul in still retreat,
And at the touch of memory, it seems
They call thee back, oh, fairest of the fair,
Dear summer gone for aye, but oh, how sweet !

BE KIND.

" Be kind." It seemed a little child had spoken,
As I lay dreaming there beneath the trees;
I wakened, still was echoed on the breeze,
" Be kind "—save this, the silence was unbroken.
Whence came the voice the stillness gave no token—
It seemed the distant murmur of the seas
Took up these two sweet words, yea, only these;
And now I knew the voice of God had spoken,
For wan, sad faces came, and clustering
About my heart, they entered there to find
Sweet love who came to me on golden wing,
With pity's garments clothed me, soul and mind.
Then mercy kissed my lips; I learned to sing ;
The theme of all my song is this, " Be kind."

LONGING.

WHAT art thou, O thou guest within my breast?
Thy burdened spirit wanders to and fro
As restless as the ocean's ebb and flow,
And lends my soul a spirit of unrest.
I would that thou shouldst leave me—it were best;
Thy presence as the moments come and go
Is torture,—this, and only this, I know.
Yet I have loved thee, fair, unwelcome guest,
And at thy bidding stretched my arms to find
But empty space, but falling tears and pain;
Where'er I go thou goest but to bind
Thy tyrant's cords about me—yet refrain,
I 've learned at last that thou art most unkind;
Oh, leave my heart, and ne'er come back again.

DECEIVED.

To-day I sit alone, awake, yet dreaming;
   From out the dear dead past you come to me,
You kiss my eyes, bend over me, in seeming
   As fond as you were wont those days to be.
Your voice, your touch hath all the olden power,
   Again I tremble with exquisite pain,
And lay my lips on thine through many an hour,
   And dizzy grows my heart and soul and brain.

And is it but a dream, as I was saying,
   Or do you love me still ? It seems—but then,
What matter what it seems ?—not all the praying
   Of my poor soul can call you back again.
You seemed so constant and so true a lover,
   You scorched my very soul with passion's fire,
I thought your love matched mine, but all is over,
   My heart loves on, and you already tire.

Wherefore is love so blind ? Another loved me,
   And I—I did not care, I loved but you;

You coldly went away, perchance you proved me
 The better thus to show yourself untrue.
But why is love so blind, forever stealing
 From passions not her own her dearest bliss ?
Another would have died to kindle feeling
 Within my breast—I cursed him for your kiss.

And now—but no, I do not blame—I love you,
 I 've learned to read aright your heart and mine,
I pray the God of Love keep watch above you,
 My heart hath learned to pray, I do not pine.
I warmed your passions by my own so tender,
 I taught you to respond—O God ! believed
That that was love in all its bliss, its splendor;
 You thought it too—we both have been deceived.

THE FIRST-BORN.

SOFTLY, my dear one, baby is sleeping;
Gaze thou upon him, but kiss me instead,
Lest he awaken.   Oh, priceless treasure,
Pledge of our happiness, union, and love!
How like thyself is our little one; dearer
Each day he grows, as I trace in his face
Features like thine; when his blue eyes are open
Almost I can read in their depth thine own soul.
What shall we name him ?   What, love, is thy name ?
Is there another so sweet to my ear ?
Like thee thy babe in name and in feature—
That he shall be like thee, noble and true,
Kneel by his cot, love, and help me to pray.
So thou shalt bless for the gift I have given,
When we shall kiss o'er the gulf of the years.
I opened my arms, Thou gavest this treasure,
Blest God, in Thy goodness, mercy, and love;
And, oh, that the little feet ne'er go astray,
The soul of our babe be kept white as the snow,
We kneel down together and fervently pray.

SONNET.

If thou hadst been as others are, in vain
Had been thy passion—from thee I could go,
And could forget.   Ah, it were best, I know,
To say good-bye and leave thee—but this pain,
This misery of heart and soul and brain
Is sweet if I may see thy face, and so
For this I stay, though it were best to go—
Aye, best and right that we ne'er meet again.
But, love, through all the long remorseless years,
Apart from thee my heart must sorely ache;
'T is sweet to see thy face e'en through my tears,
'T is sweet to love e'en tho' the heart must break.
Yet, if 't is sin, and we must say good-bye,
Ah, God be merciful to me, and let me die.

LIKE THE STRINGS OF THE OLD GUITAR.

An old guitar on a table lay,
  In a room that was dark and still,
And the twilight shades at the close of day
  Filled the room with gloom until,
As the soft winds sighed through the open door,
  Like a breath from worlds afar,
They struck one chord that was wondrous sweet
  From the strings of the old guitar.

And I seemed to see in the far-off past,
  Where my youth and dreams both perished,
A life made glad with the dreams made real,
  With the gifts and joys so cherished.
And I looked again, and a life I saw
  Void of sin and selfish pleasure,
Tho' in this fair life not a dream came true,
  And the years gave naught to treasure.

Then the night shades fell—like a great black sea
  Did the darkness float around me,

While the idols torn from a chastened heart
  Seemed to rise like ghosts about me.
Then I knew the gift that is best of all
  Is the peace that naught can mar—
Oh, respond, my heart, to the breath of good
  Like the strings of the old guitar.

REGRET.

WOULD that on mine no other lips had rested,
  Would that no hand save thine had dared caress,
Would that no thrill of passion or of pleasure
  Had pierced my heart or given happiness!
Ah, then the past, the present, and the future,
  A gift most sweet I 'd gladly give to thee,
And now I should be blessed if ne'er another
  Had loved me or had sailed with me life's sea.

If to thine heart so true I came from heaven,
  If to thy lips I brought an angel's kiss,
Then were I worthy—then, my God, I 'd lay me
  Sweetly to rest within the arms of bliss.
Then would I bid thee take my heart and hide it
  Safely forever—it were then thine own;
Ah, if 't were true I ne'er had loved another,
  No other loved me, called me his alone!

Yet with my soul I have not loved; oh, ever
  True love has slumbered in my heart of pain;

But now, awakened, echoes and re-echoes,
  Haunting the soul forever and in vain:
Would I could rest within thine arms so tender,
  Weep on thy breast these tears of pain! and yet,
Now that I love and truly, all unworthy,
  Nothing is mine but weeping and regret.

WE WERE SCHOOLMATES, FRED AND I.

We kissed good-bye, I went away,
   He twined a wreath about my head,
A wreath of snowy roses—yea,
   And mixed with passion roses red.
" I will be true," each softly said,
   And then once more we kissed good-bye;
We were too young, 't is true, to wed,
   But we were schoolmates, Fred and I.

What matters all the rest ?   I say,
   What if we did forget ? and Fred,
As men will do, forgot to pray,
   Thus did he with another wed.
The long, long years went by; unfed,
   My childish fancy could but die,
Neglected in its garden-bed—
   But we were schoolmates, Fred and I.

I wandered back at last—to-day
   We meet again, the roses red

Are blooming as of yore.   Ah, may
　　Their grace delight as they are spread
For her he loves; oh, may she tread
　　Where flowers greet a cloudless sky.
We part once more as from the dead—
　　But we were schoolmates, Fred and I.

ENVOY.

O days of youth, so quickly fled,
　　Ye mock me with your cruelty;
We close the book, the tale is read—
　　But we were schoolmates, Fred and I.

ABIDE WITH ME.

WHEN the flowers bloom about me,
   When the sun lights up the sky,
When the birds are sweetly singing,
   When no evil thing is nigh,
Fold me in Thine arms, dear Saviour,
   Hold me closer, Lord, to Thee,
While the flowers bloom about me,
   Father, O abide with me !

When the night falls dark about me,
   Clouds have gathered in the sky,
When the birds have ceased their singing,
   When the blossoms droop and die,
Yet shall I sing on as gladly,
   Though Thy face I may not see,
If Thine arms of love enfold me.
   Father, O abide with me!

Yes, abide with me, my Saviour;
   Every joy would lose its sweet

If I wander from Thy presence—
　O, I pray Thee, guide my feet!
Yea, Thy word shall light my pathway,
　Give me life and love and Thee,
Thou hast said Thou 'lt ne'er forsake me,
　Evermore abide with me !

THANKSGIVING.

THAT I may weep with those who needs must weep,
May scatter sunbeams o'er some darkened way;
That I may hope and sing, may love and pray,
And cheer the faint while careless millions sleep;
That I may sail the ocean grand and deep
Of God's great love, and know that day by day
He leadeth me in whom I trust alway,—
What though the path be thorny, rough, and steep?
If I may plant a rose where thistle grew,
One weary head may pillow on my breast,—
Enough to tread where bleeding feet have trod,
Enough to know that all my soul is true—
For all of these, for mercy, peace, and rest,
Thanksgiving, praise, and honor to our God.

TOO SWEET THE PAST.

Too sweet the past, and thou too dear
To be forgot; oh, love, how drear
　　The future years will be, and when
　　In dreams thy lips touch mine again—
God pity me! through many a year
I 'll hunger for thy touch, and clear
As chiming bells thy voice I 'll hear;
　　Oh, I shall thirst—'t is true hath been
　　　　Too sweet the past.

Out on life's sea we learned to steer
Our boats to meet, yet now the spear
　　Hath entered both our hearts; and then
　　We may not hope to meet again,
Our cup o'erflowed—'t is true, my dear,
　　　　Too sweet the past.

NO OTHER LOVE.

THOU 'RT not the first to love me,
　　The last thou may'st not be,
And yet my heart is faithful, dear,
　　No other love for me.
O sweet past! forever
　　With thee I shall rove,
And drink from life's fountains
　　No other love.

Thy love hath been the sweetest
　　My soul hath known—ah, me !
I would not give those days of bliss
　　For all eternity.
Belov'd past, thy pleasures
　　Had wings of the dove ;
O sweet past! there is for me
　　No other love.

ANGELS' VOICES.

WE 'VE heard them at morning, at noonday,
    And oft in the still of the night,
The silver-toned voices of angels—
    And almost their wings, snowy white,
Have brushed us in passing, and ever
    We welcome the heavenly guests
That beckon us onward and upward,
    Where God, the great Infinite, rests.

Sometimes when the soul grows a-weary,
    The angel of memory wakes
The heart to its sweet olden hunger,
    And dreams of despair it forsakes.
Perchance it is only a footstep
    That fell on the listening ear,
And echoed the one stilled forever,
    Remembered with many a tear.

It may be when hushed into slumber,
    That loved lips are pressed close to thine,

The dream angel hovers about thee,
   And voices a carol divine.
It may be the scent of a flower,
   That bloomed while the stars brightly shone,
While hope sang her sweetest—this only,
   And yet it hath sweetness unknown.

And so all about us are angels,
   And he who will listen may hear
The voices so tender and holy
   That wait for the listening ear.
We live, and the forms we have cherished
   Pass onward and out of our sight,
But the voices, sweet voices, remind us
   That over the way there 's no night.

THE LEAVES OF THE ROSES OF LOVE.

Long after the beautiful roses
   Have melted away in decay,
The leaves grace the bush in the garden—
   The leaves!—and we welcome their stay.
So after the bright dream of passion
   Has faded, its short life to prove,
Comes friendship to soften the sorrow—
   The leaves of the roses of love.

But love that is sweetest and dearest,
   Fades not like the red passion rose,
And builded on friendship, forever
   The flame in its strength hotter glows.
The bright stars ne'er fail us at twilight,
   And ever the heavens are blue,
The white rose of love never withers
   For hearts that are faithful and true.

FRAGMENTS.

How little, at the best, we know our friends;
How little of their inmost lives we know;
We see the smile, but do not guess the tear
That waits the precious hour of solitude.
Ah, could we read the struggles of the heart
And know how fierce the war with sin, and how
We blame where just and right would be our praise,
Methinks the heart of man would be more kind
To those who fall.   In pity's garments dressed,
We each and all would lend a helping hand,
The unkind word forever be unsaid.

Once when a child, while roaming o'er the prairie
And plucking sweet wild flowers, I spied a plant
All pink and white, so beautiful and dainty;
I sought to break it from its stem, but, lo!
I did but touch it ere it drooped and died.
I find some natures so—unloved they perish,
They droop, they fade away before our eyes;   ·
Some guard the jewel, others prize the casket,
And so the hands toil on, the heart may break.

YE MEMORIES!

O YE memories! ye voices of the past!
Why do ye haunt my solitude ?   I pray
Give—give the joys with which ye tempt my soul,
Or leave me, and forevermore be gone!
Sometimes 't is but a word I chance to hear,
'T is only this—a word—ye come! ye come!
Ye memories, and oh, I do so long
For all ye mock me with,—once more to hear
A well-known footstep and a voice whose tones
Had power to wake my soul.   And then, ofttimes
When I had schooled my thought e'en to forget,
And lay me down to rest with less of pain,
In dreams, ye cruel memories, ye come!
Again I feel his hot lips press my own.
O God! I can but creep into his arms
And drink with him the pure delights of love,
And, in my dreams all other things forgot,
We need not part as now ; I hold him close,
For there 's no other lives who claims my life,
No law of God or man forbids our love.
And then I wake from dreaming: O my God!

It seems I cannot—cannot let thee go!
Gaston, O Gaston! for one hour as sweet
As that in which I dreamed, thy lips on mine,
My head upon thy breast, thy form close pressed,
Had I a million lives to give, that hour
Should purchase all—and yet, I bade thee go,
And never, never shall I call thee back.
Ye memories, be gone! ye drive me mad!
I love the pain ye give more than sweet peace,
And yet, but to remember—ah, 't is sin;
I hunger to forget.   Some seek to still
Thy voice—'t is that remembrance brings remorse;
In rioting and sin some fain would find
Release from thee, ye memories, and some
By thee are lifted into purer light,
Where right forever antidotes the wrong;
Some curse thee, others cherish thee, and I—
I love thee well—'t is sin; I bid thee go!

MY BABY GIRL.

THE eve before her wedding-day
I kissed her when we knelt to pray,
  And wept in silence by her side,
It seemed my heart could only say
  " To-morrow she will be a bride."
  My tear-stained face I sought to hide,
She was so happy, bright, and gay,
  The words I spoke my heart belied.

This little girl of mine, ah me,
Who oft has sat upon my knee,
  And kissed my lips and pulled my hair,
Shall soon be gone—oh, can it be ?
  I looked into her face so fair,
  So free from pain and blight of care,
Her heart I knew was glad and free,
  Yet seek her eyes I did not dare.

The years rolled by and then I knew
God blessed her with a daughter, too;

I held the wee one to my breast,
I kissed her laughing eyes of blue,
 And then my aching heart found rest,
 So welcome was the little guest,
My heart to her was wondrous true,
 They brought her to the old home nest.

And all the day she 'd laugh and sing,
And flit about like bird of wing,
 This little granddaughter of mine,
This tiny, precious, pretty thing,
 Whose every move I thought divine;
 About my neck her arms she 'd twine
Until my cares I learned to fling
 Away, and watch her bright eyes shine.

Hush! do not speak, I 'll tell you all,
One day into the dim old hall
 They bore a tiny casket white,
And baby went, beyond recall,
 To where 't is true all things are bright
 And only beauty greets the sight,
And yet—and yet the tear-drops fall
 When lone I lay me down at night.

And then—O God ! 't is hard to tell—
The mother into sickness fell—
    And soon she, too, had gone from me,
It broke my heart to say farewell.
    Then out upon death's dismal sea,
    With her loved child again to be,
She left me nothing but a knell,
    A funeral knell was left to me.

The morning light comes in my room,
The night has fled with all its gloom,
    My God! and can it be I dreamed
These visions which before me loom ?
    This thing which all so real has seemed ?
    She lies upon my breast; I deemed
Her grown to womanhood; the bloom
    Comes back to life—I only dreamed.

A NAME.

'T WAS not while the sun shone bright on high,
And the roses bloomed 'neath a smiling sky,
That the word like an angel's tear-drop came
To give to the deepest grief a name,
But just as the twilight softly fell,
And the full-blown rose was dead, a knell
Was breathed on the list'ning soul—'t was met
With a wail that echoed the word " regret."

AS WE SEE IT.

FORTH from my neighbor's house one day
　　The blue smoke issued—and horrified
Myself and my neighbors all stood by,
　　And looked and looked till we almost cried,
And the news of my neighbor's woe spread far
　　O'er the whole extent of the countryside.

Like the Pharisee self-righteous I,
　　And to prove my sinlessness I told
How smoke from my neighbor's house had burst,
　　And I added color with hand most bold;
Then back to my own home nest I flew,
　　And bolted the windows firm and fast,
Lest smoke from my home should issue too,
　　And I smiled contented when all was past.

FORGOTTEN.

ONLY a word of encouragement,
It was looked for long, but never sent.
I meant to have said it, and yet, and yet,
Why do we who mean to do well forget ?
The days rolled on like a dreamy sea,
The message he waited anxiously—
            Forgotten.

'T was only a poem, yet replete
With sentiment tender, pure, and sweet;
My tears fell fast on the dainty thing
That taught my heart like a bird to sing,
I hid it away, and then forgot
To write to my friend and knew it not—
            Forgotten.

I think that he waited many a day,
But then at the last he went away,
I knew not whither, and none else knew;
And ever, forever, my heart is true,
While over the weary waste of years
My soul still echoes amid my tears—
            Forgotten.

THEY TELL ME THOU ART GROWING OLD.

THEY tell me thou art growing old,
To say so much is over bold,
And yet perchance, it may be true
To they who know thee not—they who
Would measure life by hair grown white,
Or by the dimness of the sight.

What! is the heart less young to-day,
Because the years have sped away,
And left thee, in the place of youth,
God's benediction ? Ah, forsooth,
Thy heart a book of wisdom is,
Thy past and future both are His.

Come! fold me to thy manly breast,
There only would I seek my rest,
Breathe on my lips thy pure sweet breath,
For mine thou art until in death
We part for just a little while,
One going first beneath God's smile.

For, dear one, some would have it so—
Thou art too old for me—no, no!
The fires that in thy bosom burn
Have kindled all my soul—I turn
From loneliness to thee—oh, bind
To thine my heart and soul and mind.

And while the ages onward roll,
Hide thou rich treasure in my soul,
But look into my eyes to say:
'' My heart loves on from day to day.''
What shall I care, as years unfold,
They tell me thou art growing old ?

ALONE.

JUST as the sun went down in the west
    One beautiful summer day,
I sat in the open door to rest
    And dream, as a dreamer may.

And I said in my heart, I 'm all alone,
    I will call up visions fair.
O fate! what a sad mistake, for I
    Was alone, and grief was there.

MY LITTLE DAUGHTER.

God gave to me a jewel wondrous rare,
A priceless gem, and bade me guard with care,
A baby girl, a tiny heart and soul,
To lead as best I could home to the goal.

And I have asked my soul: " Soul, which is best
For this, my child, to enter with the rest
The strife for worldly honors, glory, fame,
Or be content to bear an humble name ? "

I know not, but to guide her is my task;
O Father, lead the way, I do but ask
That she unto the world a blessing prove,
That I may guide aright to know Thy love.

And if the way for her be dark, my plea:
Oh, grant that she may ever lean on Thee,
That she may ne'er in darkness lose her way,
Help me, O Father, teach her how to pray.

WHO ?

Who was it through that summer time,
 That summer ne'er forgot to be,
Who taught me love thro' golden hours,
 And filled my cup with joy ? 'T was he
Who colored all my thoughts to please
 His own sweet fancies as he would,
And while the days went sailing by,
 To me to live was good.

For hope was kindled into flame,
 Oh, love was as a fire
That glowed, but never could consume
 The sweetness of desire.
Somebody sent his spirit then
 To bless and make me glad,
And I, enraptured, could but yearn
 Till yearning drove me mad.

Where'er I went this spirit form
 Was with me night and day,

He kissed me in my dreams, and then
  He knelt with me to pray.
While others heard the great church choir,
  I only heard his voice,
And in the hope of meeting him,
  I learned to live, rejoice.

And then at last—at last—we met,
  My God! and could I tell
The raptures of those golden hours,
  Methinks 't would break the spell
That binds me to the past—but wait!
  You dare not ask me who
That idol of my heart was ; well,
  We 're friends to-day—'t was you!

REVENGED!

IF, in the midst of pleasure,
    Granted one's whole desire,
Counting one's wealth of treasure,
    Letting one's hopes aspire
E'en to the heights of glory,
    If in the arms of bliss
Pain mingles with the story,
    Grief in the sweetest kiss;

If, in the past remembered,
    Lingers one great regret,
Pain that for years hath slumbered,
    Tears one would hide, as yet;
If, at the hour of midnight
    Cometh remorse—O God,
Better to veil the sunlight,
    Better to kiss the rod.

Look on that form of beauty
    Asleep in the husband's arms,

Love is the work of duty—
  What can it be alarms,
Wakens her from her dreaming,
  Makes her to start in pain ?
Ah, it was but in seeming,
  For see, she smiles again.

But when her eyelids drooping,
  Lull her again to rest,
One o'er her couch is stooping,
  Kissing her lips, her breast;
Weeping great tears of sorrow,
  Calling her back to him,
She from the past would borrow
  Happiness, love, and Jim.

Yet in our dreams awaken
  Memories crushed to death,
Loves that have been forsaken,
  Scorch us with burning breath.
So in the midnight darkness,
  Back in the past she lives,
Memory robbed of sweetness,
  Never the thief forgives.

Seems now some anguished spirit,
  Hovering near in air,
Speaks, and she waits to hear it,
  Ah, it is hushed in prayer,
While in the tones of pleading
  Echoes her lover's voice,
Upward to God 't is leading;
  Fair sleeping bride, thy choice

Opened the deeps of anguish
  For one who was faithful, true,
Leave him for aye to languish,
  What can it be to you ?
Fair as the dawn of morning,
  False as the vows you take,
Shame shall be thine adorning,
  Hearts have been thine to break.

" Morning hath dawned, O fair one,
  Open thy bright blue eyes.
What! not a kiss, my dear one ?
  No wife this gift denies."
And while her lips he presses,
  Under her artful smile,
Read what her heart confesses—
  Thou art revenged the while!

CROWNED.

Crowned with a wreath of roses,
  Crowned on my bridal day,
Is there a soul supposes
  Roses will ne'er decay ?
Ah, but the sun shines brightly,
  Youth is the time to sing,
And while the roses wither,
  Zephyrs are on the wing.

Crowned as the years go onward,
  Crowned, and with motherhood,
Oft in the dark night's stillness,
  Merged into prayerful mood:
" Father," I plead, " oh, make me
  Worthy to wear this crown,
Dearer than all earth's treasure,
  And than the world's renown."

Crowned, but the roses withered,
  Leaving the thorns all bare;

Oh, wilt Thou not, dear Father,
   Help me this crown to wear ?
One in the world is tempted,
   Dear to my mother's heart,
Oh, that his steps ne'er falter,
   Help me to do my part.

One—'t was my only daughter,—
   Sank in the arms of death
Just as a tiny wee one
   Gaspingly caught its breath;
And as I kissed her forehead,
   White as the drifted snow,
I lifted her crown of roses,
   Glad that she could not know

That after the sunlit morning,
   There cometh the dews of night,
And after the roses wither,
   Tear-drops will blind the sight.
And yet, by the low mound sitting,
   The thorns do so pierce my brow,
Almost I would yield my guerdon,
   To not be a mother now.

'T is past, and again I 'm smiling,
   'T is best that a crown of thorns,
All bathed in a mother's anguish,
   My own aching brow adorns.
For out of the deeps of sorrow
   Comes healing for others' woe,
Then soul, like the Master, suffer,
   Like Him, thou shalt victory know.

DELIGHT.

I SAID, I will search, I will seek till I find
    That fairy bewitching and bright,
That dazzles the eye and entrances the mind,
    That gorgeous elf men call Delight.

I sought her in summer mid sunshine and bloom
    I sought her in winter's soft snows,
She ever evaded me, left me in gloom,
    Where is she ?   Methinks no one knows.

I thought I had found her when love left his kiss
    On hot burning lips—oh ! the might
Of feeling that trembled and thrilled at the bliss
    Of this, the first touch of Delight.

But quickly she vanished, I sat down to weep,
    The phantom I followed had fled,
And there in the twilight I fell into sleep,
    And these were the dreams of my head:

I saw the great world seeking her whom I sought,
  And men laid their wealth at her feet,
And all were bewildered, great treasure they
    brought,
  And heaped up her storehouse as meet.

Fair women laid beauty adown in the dust
  Of sin, degradation, and shame,
Believing for this that Delight would and must
  Write on them her beautiful name.

But ever I saw, let them try as they would,
  They ne'er touched the hem of her gown,
For ever and always she fled in such mood
  That none ever won the bright crown.

And then in my dreaming a vision I saw,
  Methinks 't was no dream of the night,
For there was the spirit and word of the law,
  And there was the throne great and white.

'T was set in the midst of the homes of the earth,
  And not in the far-away skies,
And Jesus, the Master, regarded the worth
  Of things that the world doth despise.

I heard a great groaning, men heartsick from sin,
   And women and children in pain,
I saw a great conflict about to begin,
   Where effort and struggle seemed vain.

And then like the angels of God forth there came,
   Fair women who knelt down to pray
Beside some poor lost one and teach him the name
   Of Christ, the Light, Truth, and the Way.

They moistened the lips of the dying with tears,
   They hushed every story of ill ;
In all that broad land sin died out with its fears,
   For tongues that spoke evil grew still.

These angels of mercy appeared at the throne,
   Were crowned and were robed in pure white,
And given a gem—'t is the rarest that 's known,
   A talisman true of delight.

I waked from my dreaming, the vision is past,
   And now I have found the true way ;
Delight to her castle invites me at last,
   Oh, teach me, fair angel, to pray.

FALSELY ACCUSED!

Accused! and at the accusation, shame
Hath clothed a life and cursed an honest name;
A soul that leaned on God it hath abused,
A soul that was to sin's foul ways unused;
And God hath looked upon that aching heart,
And numbered all the actors in the part—
      Falsely accused!

The play is on—for life is, at the best,
A drama—in which good and ill attest;
On comedy the curtain oft doth rise,
More often it is tragedy that lies
Behind the scenes—all do not read aright,
And lives are blighted that are in God's sight
      Falsely accused!

The struggle, how severe, 'twixt right and wrong!
The night of trial, oh, how fierce and long!
Almost the floating banner did go down,

And yet, and yet, remembering the crown
" To him that overcometh," grace was sought
And honor saved.　O soul, I pray, faint not—
　　　Falsely accused!

Not guilty! so the record reads above;
Not guilty! that great judgment day shall prove;
Then wait in patience while the years go by,
And pray for them who pierce thee thro'—aye,
　　aye,
Enough to know that God thy cause will plead,
And write upon thy brow that all may read—
　　　Falsely accused!

CONSCIENCE.

CONSCIENCE, what art thou ?
A tyrant thou to torture if I stray,
A demon of the night! and if I pray,
A spirit hov'ring o'er my anguished soul,
That bids me drink the dregs from out the bowl.
I sink beneath thy lash, and yet, O God,
My quivering lips would kiss Thy scourging rod.

Conscience, thou art
An angel sent to guide me thro' the dark,
Ofttimes I 'd lose my way in sin, but hark!
Thy voice is heard to speak, and then I know
The Father loves me yet—Oh, soft and low
As twilight echoes are I hear thy voice,
And ever at thy coming I rejoice.

NIGHT AND DAY.

THE dusky night, the golden day,
The dearer which I know not—yea,
Methinks the star-lit skies of blue,
While earth is bathed with falling dew,
The dearer is, yet with delight,
The daylight chases dusky night.

The while 't is day in every clime,
I seek and know the joys of time,
When night lulls me to sleep, ah, me !
I dwell within eternity;
My waking dreams are what I would,
I sleep—God giveth what is good.

The day for toil and strife at best,
The night for prayer and peace and rest,
Of all the joys I 've known, it seems,
The sweetest came to me in dreams.
And so I am rejoiced alway
That night must follow golden day.